Vampires

Fact or Fiction?

Other books in the Fact or Fiction? series:

Vampires

Fact or Fiction?

Angela Cybulski, *Book Editor*

Daniel Leone, *President*
Bonnie Szumski, *Publisher*
Scott Barbour, *Managing Editor*

OPPOSING
VIEWPOINTS®
SERIES

GREENHAVEN
PRESS®

THOMSON
————★————™
GALE

San Diego • Detroit • New York • San Francisco • Cleveland
New Haven, Conn. • Waterville, Maine • London • Munich

THOMSON

_____ ✦ _____ ™

GALE

For more information, contact
Greenhaven Press
27500 Drake Rd.
Farmington Hills, MI 48331-3535
Or you can visit our Internet site at http://www.gale.com

Cover credit: © Bettmann/CORBIS

LIBRARY OF CONGRESS CATALOGING-IN-PUBLICATION DATA

Vampires / Angela Cybulski, book editor.
   p. cm. — (Fact or fiction?)
  Includes bibliographical references and index.
  ISBN 0-7377-1316-X (lib. : alk. paper) — ISBN 0-7377-1317-8 (pbk. : alk. paper)
   1. Vampires. I. Cybulski, Angela. II. Fact or fiction? (Greenhaven Press)
  BF1556 .V34 2003
  133.4'2—dc21

                                          2002034724

Printed in the United States of America

Contents

Foreword

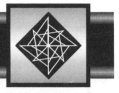

"There are more things in heaven and earth, Horatio, than
are dreamt of in your philosophy."
—William Shakespeare, *Hamlet*

"Extraordinary claims require extraordinary evidence."
—Carl Sagan, *The Demon-Haunted World*

Almost every one of us has experienced something that
we thought seemed mysterious and unexplainable. For example, have you ever known that someone was going to call
you just before the phone rang? Or perhaps you have had a
dream about something that later came true. Some people
think these occurrences are signs of the paranormal. Others
explain them as merely coincidence.

As the examples above show, mysteries of the paranormal
("beyond the normal") are common. For example, most
towns have at least one place where inhabitants believe
ghosts live. People report seeing strange lights in the sky
that they believe are the spaceships of visitors from other
planets. And scientists have been working for decades to
discover the truth about sightings of mysterious creatures
like Bigfoot and the Loch Ness monster.

There are also mysteries of magic and miracles. The two
often share a connection. Many forms of magical belief are
tied to religious belief. For example, many of the rituals and
beliefs of the voodoo religion are viewed by outsiders as
magical practices. These include such things as the alleged
Haitian voodoo practice of turning people into zombies
(the walking dead).

There are mysteries of history—events and places that have been recorded in history but that we still have questions about today. For example, was the great King Arthur a real king or merely a legend? How, exactly, were the pyramids built? Historians continue to seek the answers to these questions.

Then, of course, there are mysteries of science. One such mystery is how humanity began. Although most scientists agree that it was through the long, slow process of evolution, not all scientists agree that indisputable proof has been found.

Subjects like these are fascinating, in part because we do not know the whole truth about them. They are mysteries. And they are controversial—people hold very strong and opposing views about them.

How we go about sifting through information on such topics is the subject of every book in the Greenhaven Press series Fact or Fiction? Each anthology includes articles that present the main ideas favoring and challenging a given topic. The editor collects such material from a variety of sources, including scientific research, eyewitness accounts, and government reports. In addition, a final chapter gives readers tools to analyze the articles they read. With these tools, readers can sift through the information presented in the articles by applying the methods of hypothetical reasoning. Examining these topics in this way adds a unique aspect to the Fact or Fiction? series. Hypothetical reasoning can be applied to any topic to allow a reader to become more analytical about the material he or she encounters. While such reasoning may not solve the mystery of who is right or who is wrong, it can help the reader separate valid from invalid evidence relating to all topics and can be especially helpful in analyzing material where people disagree.

Introduction

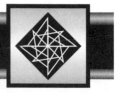

"The strength of the vampire is that people will not believe in him."

—Dr. Abraham Van Helsing, in Bram Stoker's *Dracula*

Vampire. The word conjures up a clear picture in the mind. A tall, elegantly dressed male figure, black-haired and pale-faced. Powerful and hypnotic eyes gaze out from beneath thick brows on a sinister face hiding behind a black silk cape. Cold and calculating, he quickly transforms into a bat or slowly bends to bite the neck of his current female victim.

This image of the vampire as a mysterious count lurking in the shadows, hungry for the blood of unsuspecting women, is familiar to most people. Even the dictionary defines the vampire as a corpse, or dead body, that leaves its grave at night to suck the blood of its sleeping victims. This is the vampire of horror films, scary books, and Halloween, lifeless but eternal and known to all. How did this being find such a comfortable place in our imaginations, literature, and media?

The familiar image of the vampire described here is one that has been several hundred years in the making. The vampire has existed in the cultures of most countries throughout history. Although it has appeared in locations as diverse as Greece, Asia, Europe, and Africa, it is the eyewitness accounts of the vampire that come from central and eastern Europe and the Mediterranean that are the most well known. These eyewitness accounts consistently and repeatedly describe the deaths of loved ones or townspeople who then leave their graves at night to terrorize their living family members. In his

9

book *The Vampire in Europe*, renowned vampire researcher Montague Summers suggests that eyewitnesses to vampire attacks commonly believe "vampires issue forth from their graves in the night, attack people sleeping quietly in their beds, suck out all their blood from their bodies and destroy them."[1] Several accounts describe the victim as gradually wasting away, supposedly due to loss of blood. According to Summers, even the victims themselves, "when at the point of death, have been asked if they can tell what is causing their decease, [and] they reply that such persons, lately dead, have arisen from the tomb to torment and torture them."[2] Most often, the victim in these accounts does ultimately die. In other cases, the victim is saved by intrepid vampire hunters who unearth the vampire's body and destroy it either by decapitation or by burning the vampire's heart.

Eyewitness accounts illustrate that the early encounters people had with the undead provided a range of shared experiences. These eventually allowed for the emergence of a uniformly accepted definition of the vampire as a creature who returned from the dead to feed off the blood of the living. Richard Noll, a psychiatric researcher who has done a great deal of work on the real-life implications of the mystery of the vampire, points out that the "early description[s of the vampire cited by Summers] provides all the essential characteristics of the vampire . . . as we still know it today."[3] These eyewitness accounts provide a reason for the common definition of the vampire, but they also serve to restrict and limit our view of this mysterious being. Most people take the common dictionary definition of the vampire for granted, blindly accepting the stereotype without ever bothering to look into the idea further. But is this all that there is to the mysterious identity of the vampire?

The image people most commonly associate with the vampire was likely joined to the popular definition for the first time in the nineteenth century. The sensational vampire as a bloodthirsty count was created by an Irish novelist named Bram Stoker. Many believe that, with the publication of his novel *Dracula* in 1897, Stoker single-handedly defined the image of the vampire for generations to come; even today, when people think of a vampire it is generally a caricature of his Count Dracula that they imagine.

Stoker took the raw material available from the eyewitness accounts and colored it with superstitions of his own imagining. He also very loosely based his Count Dracula on a fourteenth-century Romanian warlord by the name of Vlad Tepes (pronounced Tse-pesh), also known as Vlad Dracul ("Dragon"). Although Tepes was a very real person, he is not considered to be a vampire. He was, however, guilty of committing numerous acts of mass murder and torture. Since blood figured prominently in these acts, perhaps his reputation as a bloodthirsty scoundrel is the reason why later generations mistakenly labeled him as the father of all vampires. In fact, Vlad was a well-respected, if rightfully feared, ruler in his time.

With a few creative twists and the addition of some convincing details, Stoker came up with a fictional work of art based in fact. His vampire is based not only on the dictionary definition, which evolved from eyewitness accounts, but is also based on the historical facts of Vlad Dracul. Stoker simply added the pasty white skin, sharp fangs, garlic, crosses, capes, and castles that all became part of the commonly accepted mythology surrounding the vampire. These details still persist in contemporary fiction and film and continue to significantly influence our mental image of the vampire.

However, merging the fact-based definition with a fictional creation is problematic, mainly because it fails to provide an accurate picture of the vampire. Paul Barber is a

forensic anthropologist known for his research into the eyewitness accounts of vampires and the biological processes
of death. He points out that the appearance of the vampire
seen in the documented eyewitness accounts sharply con-
trasts the fictional vampire presented in film and literature.
Whereas the fictional vampire has pale skin, the vampire
seen by eyewitnesses "is never pale, as one would expect
from a corpse." In fact, the color of the vampire seen by eyewitnesses is often "described as florid, or . . . healthy . . . or
dark, and this may be attributed to [its] habit of drinking
blood."[4] Barber also points out that, although in film and
books "the vampire's teeth are an essential characteristic,"
the vampires reported in eyewitness accounts do not possess teeth that are "especially prominent."[5] The "typical
vampire," reported in eastern European eyewitness accounts
like the ones described by Summers, would certainly not re-
semble the Count Dracula type of vampire normally associated with the typical definition. Instead, according to Barber, the vampire seen by eyewitnesses would appear to be a
"plump Slavic fellow with long fingernails and a stubbly
beard, his mouth and left eye open, his face ruddy and
swollen. He wears informal attire—in fact, a linen shroud—
and he looks for all the world like a disheveled peasant."[6]
This image is far removed from the popular image of the
vampire that opened this argument. The inconsistencies between the commonly accepted image of the vampire and
the reality of the vampire as perceived by eyewitnesses suggests potential problems in our ability to clearly and cor-
rectly identify the real characteristics of a vampire.

The Need for a New Definition

A close examination of the origins of our common definition of the vampire indicates that the basic "fact" of the eyewitness sightings merged with the "fiction" of literature to

form a very narrow and, since it is ultimately based in a novelist's fiction, inaccurate definition of the vampire. Furthermore, this narrow definition does not provide any assistance in determining the truth behind the mystery of vampires and whether they exist. In fact, based on the popular definition alone, a majority of people would argue that vampires do not exist. Yet this argument would be flawed from the beginning since what is most commonly known of the vampire is based on the fictional image of Count Dracula and not the eyewitness sightings that first gave rise to the original definition.

Further reading of the dictionary definition presents an interesting twist to the argument in favor of a revised definition. According to the American Heritage Dictionary, a vampire can also be defined as a being that preys on others in order to survive. It does not say whether this being is alive or dead, so a vampire could just as easily be a human as a corpse. Typically, the term *prey* is associated with beasts in the wild hunting for food. The bloodsucking vampire certainly preys on living victims. However, *to prey* can also be defined as victimizing or making a profit at someone else's expense. Unfortunately, this secondary definition is all but discounted in any discussion of the vampire. Yet it is just this definition that enables a logical discussion of the vampire to move forward. It also provides a reason why it is necessary to rethink the entire definition of the vampire and the image associated with that definition.

Research in the field of vampirology (the study of vampires) suggests that vampires can inhabit a range of at least five different forms. The characteristics of these vampires can be expressed in alternative ways that challenge the stereotypes commonly associated with the dictionary definition and its companion image. If one is to determine whether vampires do exist, it would be helpful to have a clear and accurate understanding of exactly what a vampire is based on a definition that takes all of these other forms into account. A revised definition would identify the key characteristics of the vampire based on research in the field of vampirology. The type of vampire seen by eyewitnesses has already been discussed. We know that a vampire can be a reanimated, blood-drinking corpse. But as the following examples illustrate, the vampire can assume many disguises, not all of which are dead or interested in blood.

The Criminal Vampire

The criminal vampire is perhaps the type most similar to his undead counterpart. Although relatively rare, the criminal vampire is extremely dangerous. This vampire is not a corpse but a living, breathing human being who behaves in ways that are considered vampiric in light of the traditional definition of the vampire. That is, the criminal vampire shows a keen interest in blood, often drinking it, and usually kills his victims in order to obtain it. Criminal vampires are usually viewed by the public primarily as criminals. These are the mass murderers whose cases, when solved, reveal that their desire for blood was behind their compulsion to kill.

Perhaps the most notorious criminal vampire is the Countess Elizabeth Bathory, who lived in Hungary during the 1600s. Known more famously as "the Blood Countess," court records and eyewitness testimony indicate that Bathory tortured and killed over six hundred young girls in order to bathe in and occasionally drink their blood. Apparently, the countess believed that the blood would not only enable her to preserve her youthful radiance and beauty but that it would allow her to keep the alabaster skin tone she so prized.

Was Countess Bathory a vampire? According to the traditional definition alone, one would have to say that she was not. She was not undead, and her main goal was not necessarily only to drink the blood of her victims. However, if the countess is examined in light of the extended definition— as a being who victimized or preyed on others in order to survive—the question becomes more complicated. She did indeed prey on those six hundred girls in order to "survive," to preserve herself in a way that was acceptable to her. Not only did she prey on her victims, but their blood allowed Bathory to profit at their expense as well. Regardless of whether her scheme was effective, Bathory meets the second criteria of a vampire and the revised definition must then include the behaviors of the criminal vampire.

The Clinically Ill Vampire

Another type of vampire that is also very rare has existed for much longer than people can imagine. In the fields of medicine and psychiatry, "baffling case histories of persons who seem to be suffering from mysterious afflictions have been documented for thousands of years."[7] But it has been only within the last hundred years or so that the field of psychiatry has advanced enough to allow psychiatrists to make an important discovery in the field of vampirology: the ability to diagnose a mental illness called clinical vampirism, also called Renfield's syndrome. This choice of a name is another case of fiction merging with fact. Renfield is a character in Bram Stoker's novel *Dracula* who is committed to an asylum for the clinically insane. He believes he needs the blood of animals, and eventually humans, in order to survive. Clinical vampirism is a rare and complex disorder. Nearly all individuals suffering from clinical vampirism are male. Although it is not known precisely what causes the disorder, psychiatrists have been able to identify several key stages of the illness.

According to Richard Noll, the individual suffering from this disorder will usually experience some significant or "pivotal event" during childhood that usually involves the individual either bleeding from some wound or tasting blood, which the individual often finds exciting. From here, the disease will gradually become more serious as it moves through three phases. First, the individual develops auto-vampiristic tendencies while still a child. This means that he either "scrapes or cuts" his own skin to make himself bleed. He then drinks this blood and "later learn[s] how to open major blood vessels (veins, arteries) in order to drink a steady stream of blood more directly." Next comes the zoophagic (meaning "animal-eating") stage. This is the stage experienced by Renfield in Stoker's novel. In this phase, the individual will "catch and eat or drink the blood of living creatures such as insects, cats, dogs, or birds." Finally, Noll points out that "vampirism in its true form [or the behavior resembling the common definition of the vampire] is the next stage to develop—procuring and drinking the blood of living human beings." Blood may be obtained through "some sort of consensual activity, but in lust murder type cases and in other non-lethal violent crimes, the . . . vampirism may not be consensual."[8] In these cases, the individual may use aggression to obtain the blood he needs.

According to Noll, the clinical vampire often perceives blood as having life-giving powers that leave him with "an experience of well-being and empowerment" after ingesting it. The defining characteristic "is that those suffering from the disorder are *compelled* to drink blood [emphasis added]."[9] This means that they feel, perceive, or believe that they must commit an act that will enable them to ingest the blood of a living creature. Though the unfortunate individuals suffering from clinical vampirism obviously do not correspond to the common definition of the vampire, they definitely meet the second definition. In their minds, they need the blood of other human beings or animals in order to survive; thus, they absolutely prey on others.

Self-Proclaimed Vampires

More common than any of the vampires examined so far is the person who proclaims himself a vampire and chooses to live his life as a vampire. This type of vampire may appear to be a normal, functioning human being with an average, even admirable role in his social circle. This vampire might be a teacher, lawyer, stockbroker, waitress, or even a mechanic. He could be married or in a significant relationship. The one thing that makes him obviously different is that he identifies himself as a vampire and willingly accepts his need, or belief in his need, for human blood. This vampire goes on with his normal duties during the day but feeds off of the blood of willing donors at night. The vampire may believe he was born with this need for blood, or he may have developed the need for human blood after some influential experience. Whatever the case, this vampire develops a relationship of trust and openness with his blood donor, taking small amounts of blood at prearranged times, usually within the intimate setting of the donor's home. These vampires are not violent or aggressive and do not take blood against the will of the donor.

Dr. Jeanne Youngson, who is the founder and president of the Count Dracula Fan Club, has been researching individuals who fit the description of this type of vampire for more than eleven years. According to Youngson, many people who identify themselves as vampires "disclose a lack of closeness and a neediness for human connection."[10] This type of vampire describes a feeling of energy and well-being after taking blood from a donor. Strangely, donors sometimes also claim to feel energized after giving blood, an experience dissimilar to that of victims in other vampire attacks.

Is this type of vampire actually "preying" on his donor? Since there is no physical aggression on the part of the vampire and the donor is giving his blood willingly, it may not seem to be a predatory relationship. However, "preying" on another has a secondary meaning of profiting at another's expense. Since the vampire does profit from this blood transfer, it can be argued that he does indeed prey on his donor victim and thus is a vampire according to the definition's criteria.

The Psychic Vampire

The fifth and final type of vampire is the psychic vampire. Psychic vampires are perhaps the most common type of vampire found in the field of vampire studies. Matthew Bunson, author of *The Vampire Encyclopedia*, categorizes psychic vampires as "one of the most potentially dangerous of all vampire species."[11] These vampires do not survive by feeding off the blood of their victims; rather, it is the energy, or life force, of their victims that enables these vampires to survive.

According to Joe Slate, author of *Psychic Vampires*, "The psychic vampire extracts energy from another person, typically called the host victim. The results are a temporary surge of new energy for the psychic vampire and an immediate loss of energy for the unfortunate host victim."[12] Slate's choice of the word *host* to describe the victim of a psychic vampire attack is an interesting one. This word is typically used to describe the relationship between a parasite and its victim, or host. A parasite is usually considered to be a harmful organism that lives on and feeds off of another organism. A parasite can also be defined as someone who takes advantage of the generosity of another. The type of relationship that psychic vampires, and indeed all vampires, have with their victims is essentially parasitic.

Slate also suggests that the energy gain experienced by the psychic vampire is only temporary. In this way, the psychic vampire resembles his blood-drinking cousins. Any vampire's need for energy or blood is consistently growing; thus, vampires are doomed to repeat the same act through which they obtain energy, blood, or intimacy over and over again. Since the psychic vampire possesses an "inadequate internal energy system that demands life-force energy from a host victim . . . simply replenishing the deficient energy supply" by draining the host victim is not enough. Instead, the psychic vampire's need for alternative energy "becomes a controlling force that compels the vampire to [repeatedly] invade the energy systems of selected host victims."[13] This compulsion for blood or energy is a common, defining characteristic that occurs in varying degrees of intensity among each type of vampire discussed in this argument.

In some ways, psychic vampires bear little resemblance to other vampires. Since "psychic vampirism is fundamentally an energy phenomenon,"[14] it is not necessarily perceived as a physical act seen by witnesses or even immediately felt by the victim. Alternatively, vampires who drink blood might be seen by eyewitnesses and actually must engage in direct physical contact with their victims. Although the psychic vampire may choose to engage in physical contact with his victim, this is not necessary for the energy transfer to occur.

How would a victim know that he or she had been attacked by a psychic vampire? And what does this type of vampire look like? Some characteristic symptoms that indicate a psychic vampire attack has occurred include feelings of mental and physical fatigue on the part of the victim. According to Slate, this feeling can be "either constant or gradual." Victims may also experience a sense that their personal space has been violated and that there has been an "actual siphoning of energy from [their] body." Any encounter a victim has with a psychic vampire is described as "intensely exhaustive." The other physical reactions experienced by victims of a psychic vampire attack could include "dizziness, irregular heartbeat, lightheadedness, and sometimes nausea." In describing the personality and behavioral characteristics of psychic vampires that Slate has encountered in his research, he notes that some "were warm and outgoing, others were cold and withdrawn. Several viewed themselves as personally advanced and superior to others. . . . Others viewed themselves as inferior or weak. Many of them tended to be self-absorbed and immature."[15] Based on these characteristics, a psychic vampire could be just about anyone. Nina Auerbach suggests that psychic vampires "can be everything we are, while at the same time, they are fearful reminders of the infinite things we are not."[16] Ultimately, psychic vampires victimize others to get what they want. As the examples of other types of vampires have shown, this tendency toward victimization is a characteristic shared by them all.

Identifying Characteristics of Vampires

The examples and evidence presented here clearly illustrate that vampires cannot simply be defined as reanimated corpses who leave their graves at night in search of human blood. This limited definition provides no assistance in determining the truth about the identity of the vampire. It also fails to even acknowledge the unfamiliar secondary dictionary definition that serves as the basis for this argument. In order to include the range of characteristics and behaviors displayed by the vampires discussed in this argument, it is essential to revise and broaden the stereotypical definition of the vampire. Based on the identifying characteristics of vampires discussed here, the definition of the vampire can be revised as follows:

1. A vampire can be either living or dead. This statement includes the common definition, based on eyewitness accounts that describe a vampire as the living dead, and the secondary dictionary definition, which describes vampires as beings who prey on others in order to survive.

2. A vampire can be a being who takes blood from either humans or animals for either survival or for some personal gain. With the exception of the psychic vampire, this definition encompasses each type of vampire discussed in this argument.

3. A vampire can be a human being, or group of human beings, who feed off the psychic or emotional energy of other humans. Even though the psychic vampire has no desire for the blood of its victim, it must be noted that blood is often taken to symbolize a person's life force or life energy. We often hear the term *life's blood* related to the essential red fluid that courses through the veins of every living human. That psychic vampires subsist on the invisible psychic energy or life energy of their victims does not entirely separate them from their more bloodthirsty cousins.

4. A vampire will feel compelled, or forced, to take the blood or life energy of its victim, host, or donor. This compulsion is not always acted on violently or aggressively. But research on the types of vampires discussed in this argument indicates that each type of vampire believes that his or her survival or livelihood depends on preying on victims, who quench the thirst for blood or energy.

5. All vampires victimize or prey on others and profit at the expense of their victims. This statement brings the secondary dictionary definition to the fore, giving it the emphasis it deserves and that is so essential to a true understanding of the many faces of the vampire.

In an effort to provide reliable and accurate evidence to assist in thinking about and perhaps solving the mystery of whether vampires exist in our world, this book considers vampires that meet all of the criteria in this revised definition. Admittedly, this complicates thinking about the mystery. The revised definition forces an examination of beings that are both living and dead under the same definition. It equates evil beings that thirst for blood and kill to get it with average citizens who calmly take blood given willingly by donors. The revised definition levels the playing field for vampires, allowing them to be no more and no less than what they are. Whereas on one level this may simplify things, it also stretches the boundaries of reason, demonstrating how essential a comprehensive and accurate definition is to a careful evaluation of the evidence.

Notes

1. Montague Summers, *The Vampire in Europe: True Tales of the Undead.* New York: Gramercy Books, 1996, p. 157.

2. Summers, *The Vampire in Europe,* p. 157.

3. Richard Noll, *Vampires, Werewolves, and Demons: Twentieth-Century Reports in the Psychiatric Literature.* New York: Bruner/Mazel, 1992, p. 8.

4. Paul Barber, *Vampires, Burial, and Death: Folklore and Reality.* New Haven, CT: Yale University Press, 1988, p. 41.

5. Barber, *Vampires, Burial, and Death,* p. 44.

6. Barber, *Vampires, Burial, and Death,* p. 2.

7. Noll, *Vampires, Werewolves, and Demons,* p. xv.

8. Noll, *Vampires, Werewolves, and Demons,* pp. 18–19.

9. Noll, *Vampires, Werewolves, and Demons,* pp. 18–19.

10. Quoted in Norine Dresser, *American Vampires: Fans, Victims, and Practitioners.* New York: W.W. Norton, 1989, p. 41.

11. Matthew Bunson, *The Vampire Encyclopedia.* New York: Gramercy Books, 1993, p. 215.

12. Joe H. Slate, *Psychic Vampires: Protection from Energy Predators and Parasites.* St. Paul: Llewellyn, 2002, p. 37.

13. Slate, *Psychic Vampires,* p. 41.

14. Slate, *Psychic Vampires,* p. 25.

15. Slate, *Psychic Vampires,* pp. 37, 48–49, 55.

16. Nina Auerbach, *Our Vampires, Ourselves.* Chicago: University of Chicago Press, 1995, p. 6.

Chapter 1

Fact or Fiction?

Vampires Among Us: Arguments for the Existence of Vampires

In Defense of Vampires

John V.A. Fine Jr.

John V.A. Fine Jr. is a historian from the University of Michigan and has served as a North American member of the editorial board for the *East European Quarterly*, from which the following article was excerpted. His research indicates that belief in vampires has existed for many years in various Eastern European countries, including Serbia, which is the setting for the incidents related in this article. The eyewitness accounts Fine translates illustrate the strength of the popular belief that vampires could rise up out of their graves at night to terrorize and feed upon individuals and even whole towns. Readers should be aware that a belief in vampires was not reserved for the peasants of the lower classes; religious and political leaders also believed in these creatures. Through the translation of Serbian eyewitness accounts, Fine illustrates the difficulty, and ultimate failure, political and religious leaders experienced in trying to control violent local reaction to vampires.

To start a discussion of vampires in Serbia during the first reign of Prince Miloš Obrenović (1815–39) it makes sense to describe how the Serbs of the time saw them. This can best be done by quoting the description of vampires presented by a contemporary Serb, who among his varied talents was a fine ethnographer [one who studies the cultural and socioeconomic history of societies], Vuk Karadžić:

> A man into whom (according to popular tales) forty days after death a devilish spirit enters and enlivens (making him vampirized) is called a vukodlak. Then the vukodlak comes out at night from his grave and strangles people in their houses and drinks their blood. An honest man cannot vampirize, unless some bird or other living creature flies or jumps across his dead body. Thus everywhere people guard their dead [pre-burial] to see that nothing jumps over them. Vukodlaks most often appear in the winter (particularly between Christmas and Spasovdan [a moveable feast, 40 days after Easter]). When a large number of people begin to die in a village, then people begin to blame a vukodlak from the grave (and in some places begin to say that he was seen at night with his shroud over his shoulders) and begin to guess who it might be. Then they take a black stallion without any spots or marks to the graveyard and lead it among the graves where it is suspected there are vukodlaks, for they say that such a stallion does not dare to step over a vukodlak. When they find the grave of someone they believe or guess to be a vukodlak, then they collect all the peasants and, taking with them a white thorn (or hawthorn) stake (because he fears only a white thorn stake . . .), dig up the grave; and if they find in it a man who has not disintegrated, then they pierce it with that stake and throw it on a fire to be burned. They say that when they find such a vukodlak in a grave, he is fat, swollen and red with human blood ('red as a vampire'). A vukodlak sometimes returns to his wife (especially if she is young and pretty) and sleeps with her, and they say a child born of such a union has no bones. And in times of hunger vampires often gather near mills and around granaries. They

say that all of them go with their shrouds over their shoulders. A vampire can also pass through the smallest hole, that is why it does not help to lock a door against them any more than it does against a witch.

Other collections of folk beliefs show variations. Evil people may turn into vampires as a result of their evil lives. Usually vampirization occurs forty days after death, but in certain places the transformation occurs immediately. In some places a child of a vampire and a human woman appears normal; however, he has special talents, one of which often is the ability to be a vampirdžije or vampire-finder.

Now having seen how the Serbs viewed vampires, let us turn to the sources and see the creatures in action and the responses they elicited.

Account #1: Prince Miloš and the Vampire

On 8 March 1820 various kmetovi (local elders) and other merchants of Ub wrote Prince Miloš that over the last few days people had begun to die off like flies owing to a vampire, as a result people were gathering three to one house not daring to go out at night owing to fear. So they begged the vladika (bishop), who had come to collect Church taxes [mirija], to allow them to dig up the graveyard, but he had not allowed them to do this. So they went to [the local governor, Miloš' brother] Lord Jevrem, but he without the vladika's approval was not able to give them permission. So now they begged Prince Miloš to either allow them to dig up the graveyard or to move, because they could no longer endure it.

On 10 March Miloš replied to the obština of Ub that they might open the graves, which they suspected had vampires, to seek confirmation of their suspicions [he uses the negative term superstition here], but they were forbidden to inflict any injury on the corpses; rather they were to summon the parish priest or the vladika to then read over them the prayers for the dead according to the [Church] law.

This half-way permission was sufficient for the peasants to follow their own bent, as is seen from a letter of 7 April 1820 that Jevrem wrote to his brother Miloš. Jevrem reports that he summoned the people of Ub and inquired how things were going with the vampire that had appeared among them; he learned that they had acted on their own without any cleric present. Instead they had called an elder from Panjuha who had taught them how to deal with vampires. Under his guidance they had excavated the suspect graves, piercing one body with a stake and chopping off its head which was then placed at its feet; and now the graves stood open. In one case dogs had dragged out one woman's corpse, eating it.

This was not Miloš' only vampire concern of that time. For on 5 April 1820 he expelled from Požarevac a vampirdžije (a vampire-finder) who had been familiar with vampires in Smederevo. And on 20 April he released from jail a certain vampirdžije named Ilija from village Duaka with a warning that if in the future he dug up any more vampires in any village he would be sentenced to a separation from his family and would remain in jail for good. The prince's actions against vampire-finders show that, as he had done in Ub, in regard to them, he tried to follow Church law and use prayers rather than mutilation techniques. . . .

Account #2: The Church Takes Extreme Measures

On 15 August 1836 Jovan Obrenović informed his brother Miloš that the peasants of village Svojdrug, without the knowledge of the authorities, that July, had got together and declared Miloš Raković from their village, who had died on the last Little Spasovdan [a moveable feast, falling on the first Thursday after Spasovdan], a vampire; they had dug him up, verified their beliefs in some way, and had reburied him. A short time later they informed their priest, Zaharija, about it, and he, like the rest, superstitious, went with them to Miloš' grave, where for a second time they dug him up. The priest poured holy water on him and they buried him again. Three days later the villagers again gathered and together with the village elder [kmet] Aćim Milošević, went to Miloš' grave and for a third time dug it up; they shot the corpse through, cut off his head, and again buried him.

On 28 March 1838 Timok Bishop Dositej Novaković wrote the prota [first priest] of Negotin that he had sent the protojerej of his diocese, Paun Radosavljević, and the priest of the village of Radujevac, Joan Matejić, to the monastery of St. Roman for a time—a common penalty for ecclesiastical misdemeanors—because they had allowed the villagers of Radujevac to dig up a corpse they believed to be a vampire. The first of April he wrote again to the prota of Negotin saying that he had learned that some protojerej in Negotin [surely the protojerej accused in the first letter] through the local priest had authorized the local villagers to dig up the grave of a man they had declared a vampire and to pour holy oil on him. With this permission the villagers, led by their priests, openly dug up a corpse which had died a short time before. After the priests said their prayers over the dead man, they went home, and then the villagers cut up the dead body and poured barley and boiled wine into its intestines so it would no longer vampirize and then reburied it. The bishop called on the prince to take strict action against priests participating in such affairs in order to eliminate such superstititions. . . .

Account #3: The Monk's Experience

One final event of interest, occurring during Miloš' reign, but in territory to the south of his principality and still under the

Turks, near Monastery Dečani, is described by Joakim Vujić. The conversation between himself and two monks, which he presents in dialogue form, occurred in 1826:

> During my visit to this monastery [Monastery Klisura] there was staying one old monk, named Gerasim, who was from the monastery of Dečani, but who had just been in Bosnia to seek alms. . . . And thus Father Visarion, abbot and host, gave us both dinner. And after we had dined, the following conversation occurred among the three of us.
>
> *Gerasim:* Dear brothers, can you imagine what happened two months ago in a village near Novi Pazar?
>
> *I:* And what happened, holy father? Come tell us.
>
> *Gerasim:* It happened that they dug up a vampire.
>
> *I:* And what did they do with him?
>
> *Gerasim:* What did they do? Why they ran him through with a hawthorn stake.
>
> *I:* If that is what they did, it would have served them better to have gone to the tavern to drink raki, and to have left the dead body to sleep in peace.
>
> *Gerasim:* And why leave the corpse in peace?
>
> *I:* Because in this world there are no vampires.
>
> *Gerasim:* There you are, just like our students nowadays. They don't believe in anything.
>
> *Visarion:* Sir, I beg you not to speak in that way. How can you say there are no vampires in this world?
>
> *I:* Because it is an impossible being. And I can't allow such a remark to pass with a clear conscience. But I beg you, Father Visarion, tell me, have you ever with your own eyes seen one?
>
> *Visarion:* It is true that I have never seen one, but it is what people say.
>
> *Gerasim:* But I have seen one with my own eyes; what do you say to that?
>
> *I:* Then I beg you, Father Gerasim, tell me what this vampire that you saw with your own eyes looked like.

Gerasim: What it looked like! When they dug it up, it was not decomposed, its eyes were staring and its teeth were showing and clenched.

I: And what did this, your vampire, do?

Gerasim: And what did it do! At night he went about the village, scaring and strangling people; why he went into his own house and even slept with his wife.

I: Ha ha ha! He was a crude vampire, shame on him! To even have a woman on his mind. And what did his wife do, did she chase him out?

Gerasim: Of course not; she didn't dare, because he would have strangled her.

I: Tell me more, what else happened with your vampire?

Gerasim: What happened! When they dug him up, then Priest Stavro took a hawthorn stake, forced it between his teeth, and then took a piece of holy wood and put it between his teeth and along the holy wood poured into his mouth three drops of holy water and. . . .

I: Now stop! I beg you, Father Gerasim, why didn't this vampire leap up and grab Priest Stavros by his beard?

Gerasim: You're again talking nonsense! How could he grab him by his beard, when during the day he is dead and has no strength; it is only at night that he gets power from the Unclean One, and comes to life, and then he goes about the village causing all sorts of chaos and misfortune.

I: Hmmm, so this vampire is dead in the day, but alive at night. I still just can't believe it. But tell me, what happend with your vampire in the end?

Gerasim: What happened! Why, after that, the elder Petko took that same hawthorn stake and stabbed him through the breast, and blood issued from his mouth and that was the end of him. Then they again buried him in the ground, and after that he never again left his grave, nor scared nor strangled people in the village. . . .

I, having listened to these words of the Monk Gerasim about the vampire, began to say to myself: God All-blessed! How can this people live in such error, ignorance, and superstition; and if a clergyman believes and talks such superstition, what will the common people think and say? And then casting my glance upward, said: All powerful God, give our lord Miloš a long and successful life that he may during his reign establish schools with talented teachers who can wipe out error and enlighten our people. And then I turned to the monk and in this way spoke to him.

I: Holy father, I from my side beg and advise you for God's sake not to believe that there are such monsters in this world as vampires, which could bring upon other men such injuries and misfortune, but the whole thing is only one simple and stupid superstition which does not serve any good purpose. And, tell me, Father Gerasim, what would you say if I said that even though you dug up your alleged vampire and found him not decomposed with staring eyes and clenched teeth, that that still does not prove he was a vampire. And why not? That is because in some places is found earth which is salt-sulphur (salitro-sumporita), that is it is such that when you put a dead body, in which there is still considerable blood to be found, in such ground, then the blood will coagulate and the body will swell and the earth will not allow the body to decompose, but will keep it as firm as if it were magnetic iron. And such a dead body may for 77 or more years remain undecomposed in such ground. And if we want to decompose such a body we do not need a hawthorn stake nor a priest with holy wood and water, for there is no need to torture the corpse, but one need only dig it up, take it out of the ground into the air and let it lie there for only half an hour in the air and then put it back in the grave and cover it. Then after three days dig up the corpse again and you will see that it is already half disintegrated.

And now I will tell you briefly from where vampires and such superstititions originate: From no where else but the imagination and craftiness of men. . . .

The Belief Lives On

The documents cited in my text show that vampire beliefs were widespread in Serbia at this time. They were not limited to the ignorant peasantry but were also widespread

among the clergy. Among Serbs the main issue was not
whether or not there were vampires—for Miloš himself in
not denying their existence may well not have been sure of
this himself—but how was one to deal with them; should
one use traditional village methods or should one take a
more spiritual approach and call on the clergy to eliminate
them through prayers? It would take many decades and the
establishment of schools throughout Serbia—a task begun
with vigor by Miloš—to embue people with Vujić's sceptical
rejection. In fact, even today in modern Yugoslavia such beliefs have not been entirely eradicated.

Grave Discoveries: The Story of Peter Plogojowitz

Manuela Dunn Mascetti

Manuela Dunn Mascetti is well versed in subjects that have mythological origins: In addition to *Vampire: The Complete Guide to the World of the Undead*, from which the following eyewitness account is excerpted, Mascetti has also written *The Song of Eve*, an illustrated exploration of the myth of the goddess. In the piece included here, Mascetti provides authentic documentation of the famous Slavic vampire Peter Plogojowitz. The official military report of Plogojowitz's vampiric activities details how, ten weeks after his death, he returned to claim the lives of nine other people in his village of Kisilova. Plogojowitz's return from the dead incited a panic among the townspeople, who believed that Plogojowitz's intent was to destroy the entire village. The report goes on to discuss how the initially skeptical military and religious officials governing the town eventually joined with the townspeople to exhume and destroy Plogojowitz's mys-

Manuela Dunn Mascetti, *Vampire: The Complete Guide to the World of the Undead*. New York: Viking Penguin, 1992. Copyright © 1992 by Manuela Dunn Mascetti. Reproduced by permission.

teriously fresh and vivid corpse. While this eyewitness account of Plogojowitz is widely published and studied, Mascetti's handling of it here is unique. Her critical evaluation of the evidence presented in the report provides one way for readers to model their own inquiries of the evidence presented in this text as they attempt to determine whether or not vampires exist.

A long time before vampires filled the pages of romantic horror stories, such as Bram Stoker's *Dracula*, and became so popular as to be portrayed in both fiction and movies, they are said to have plagued rural villages in those lost corners of eastern Europe such as the provinces of Hungary, Romania, and Transylvania. The popular depiction of a vampire, the one that is familiar to our imagination, is of a tall, very thin, aristocratic man. He is dressed in a black suit and a long, enveloping black cape. As a concession to his origin the outfit of the classic vampire may be a little dusty and worn-looking—having seen better days—but he is essentially an elegant character who, at first glance, we might not discard out of hand. However, on slightly closer examination we find that his irksome smile reveals protuberant, exaggeratedly long, and extremely sharp canine teeth. His breath is foul; his nails long and crooked like the fangs of a beast; his complexion so pale he looks as if he has just arisen from the grave.

But is this how the vampires that are said to have haunted villages really looked? Not at all. In fact, for the sake of the watchful, it is now important to look at a very different form of vampire from our rather grotesque but essentially elegant movie character—one that stalked the country lanes and fields of the distant past—a creature that may still be present in our darker regions. The following are eyewitness reports and give us the very best sources of proof.

Eyewitness Account

The story of Peter Plogojowitz dates back to 1725 and was witnessed by German military officials stationed in the village of Kisilova, in the Rahm District, now Slavia. Kisilova was actually in Serbia, although, because of the confused political situation of the time, it has often been reported as being part of Hungary.

Our subject, Peter Plogojowitz had died ten weeks past. He had been buried according to the Raetzian custom, a local religious ritual of the time. It was revealed that in this same village, during a period of a week, nine people, both old and young, had also died after suffering a 24-hour illness. Each of them had publicly declared, "that while they were yet alive, but on their death-bed, the above mentioned Plogojowitz, who had died ten weeks earlier, had come to them in their sleep, laid himself on them, and throttled them, so that they would have to give up the ghost."

Others who heard these reports were naturally very distressed by them, and their belief in the authenticity of them was strengthened even more by the fact that Peter Plogojowitz's wife, after saying that her husband had come to her and demanded his *opanki*, or shoes, had left the village of Kisilova.

> And since with such people (which they call vampires) various are to be seen—that is, the body undecomposed, the skin, hair, beard, and nails growing—the subjects resolved unanimously to open the grave of Peter Plogojowitz and to see if such above-mentioned signs were really to be found on him. To this end they came here to me and, telling of these events, asked me and the local pope, or parish priest, to be present at the viewing. And although I at first disapproved, telling them that the praiseworthy administration

should first be dutifully and humbly informed, and its exalted opinion about this should be heard, they did not want to accommodate themselves to this at all, but rather gave this short answer: I could do what I wanted, but if I did not accord them the viewing and the legal recognition to deal with the body according to their custom, they would have to leave house and home, because by the time a gracious resolution was received from Belgrade, perhaps the entire village—and this was already supposed to have happened in Turkish times—could be destroyed by such an evil spirit, and they did not want to wait for this.

A Skeptic Sees and Believes

Since I could not hold these people from the resolution they had made, either with good words or with threats, I went to the village of Kisilova, taking along the Gradisk pope, and viewed the body of Peter Plogojowitz, just exhumed, finding, in accordance with thorough truthfulness, that first of all I did not detect the slightest odor that is otherwise characteristic of the dead, and the body, except for the nose, which was somewhat fallen away, was completely fresh. The hair and beard—even the nails, of which the old ones had fallen away—had grown on him; the old skin, which was somewhat whitish, had peeled away, and a new one had emerged from it. The face, hands, and feet and the whole body were so constituted, that they could not have been more complete in his lifetime. Not without astonishment, I saw some fresh blood in his mouth, which, according to the common observation, he had sucked from the people killed by him. In short, all the indications were present that such people (as remarked above) are said to have. After both the pope and I had seen this spectacle, while people grew more outraged than distressed, all the subjects, with great speed, sharpened a stake—in order to pierce the corpse of the deceased with it—and put this at his heart, whereupon, as he was pierced, not only did much blood, completely fresh, flow also through his ears and mouth, but still other wild signs (which I pass by out of high respect) took place. Finally, according to their usual practice, they burned the often-mentioned body . . . to ashes of which I inform the most laudable Administration, and at the same time would like to request, obediently and humbly, that if a mistake was made in this matter, such is to be attributed not to me but to the rabble, who were beside themselves with fear.

Some Important Differences

This lengthy account, written in the style characteristic of bureaucratic eastern Europe of the eighteenth century, reveals that the vampire, Peter Plogojowitz, was an ordinary peasant of the village of Kisilova. Unfortunately, the account does not tell us anything about his personality or physical characteristics before his death, but it is quite clear from the description that he was not from aristocratic stock, nor was he wearing a long black cape and a black tuxedo in his coffin—hardly details that would have been overlooked.

The account illustrates quite clearly the difference, at least in appearance, between the fictional and the folkloric vampire. The former, as we have already described, is elegant, aristocratic, and eccentric, with the grotesque aspect of his nature only visible beneath the outer glamor at second glance. The latter is perhaps more treacherous still for he is very like you and me and to be found among us among the millions of people who inhabit the earth.

Analyzing the Evidence

It seems important, therefore, to proceed to examine very carefully the characteristics of Peter Plogojowitz as described, so that we may become familiar with the vampire species in all its potential forms. We can start by examining, through extract from the authentic report, some classic motifs of vampirism.

1. It might seem, on closer examination of the quoted report, that vampirism occurs as an epidemic. Evidence of this arises from the fact that first Peter Plogojowitz died and that within a week of his death, nine people, both old and

young, also died, in each case of a sudden 24-hour illness. Peter Plogojowitz is held responsible for the deaths of the other nine people, just as a victim of an epidemic illness, such as the plague, might have been held responsible for the deaths of his fellow villagers. In light of modern medicine we might dismiss such an idea right away, but maybe this is the mistake of "rational" man—always using "concrete" evidence when mystery is lurking just beneath the surface, eating away at certainty. To the peasant, always aware of magic, vampirism was an epidemic. One vampire caused another vampire, who in turn caused a third, and so on. If they didn't move fast to rid themselves of this plague, then all their neighbors and friends would go the same way, and the village would soon spread its infection to the town, to the country, and eventually the world would be populated by the walking dead. This must have been the ultimate fear of those subjected to such experiences as that of the presence of Peter Plogojowitz. This fear still exists in the mind and memory of mankind, evidenced by short stories such as "Place of Meeting" by Charles Beaumont (1953) and still more recent stories and movies depicting the presence of the living dead in various forms.

2. The vampire leaves his grave at night, appears before his victims and either sucks blood or strangles them. This kind of vampire is known to experts as the *ambulatory* type and is the most common vampire of all.

3. The body is said to be "completely fresh": the nose, however, has fallen in, although the hair, beard and nails have grown and new skin has formed under the old. This is an important characteristic of vampires: they do not appear dead when exhumed. On the contrary, they show signs of rejuvenation.

4. The body has no foul odor. But this may not necessarily be typical of vampirism. An eighteenth-century eccle-

siast [a member of the clergy], Don Calmet, observed that "when they (vampires) have been taken out of the ground, they have appeared red, with their limbs supple and pliable, without worms or decay; but not without great stench." The stench of the body is an important aspect of the nexus between vampirism and the plague—as we said before, in European folklore vampires cause epidemics. Foul smells were commonly associated with disease, even with the cause of disease. It was not unreasonable to imagine that as corpses smelled bad, bad smells must be a cause of disease and death. In order to combat such smells, strong-smelling substances such as aromatic softwoods, juniper, and ash were introduced. Vampirism, therefore, was believed to be catching.

5. We should note perhaps the strongest evidence of Peter Plogojowitz's vampiric state—the fresh blood of victims still trickling from his mouth. Unless this was somehow planted there, it would seem hard to deny as a piece of clear proof. How many corpses manage to retain uncongealed blood on their bodies? In addition, his own blood was still fresh and uncongealed, thus also condemning him as a vampire.

6. We learn that when the villagers stake the vampire, he bleeds profusely—after several weeks in the grave. The "wild signs" that the author spares us details of probably imply that the corpse's penis was erect. The vampire is a sexual creature, and his sexuality is obsessive. In Yugoslavian legends, for example, when the vampire is not sucking blood, he is apt to wear out his widow with his attentions, so that she too pines away, much like his other victims. This also raises the question of whether the vampire's activities are always only those of blood sucking, or whether his young female victims may also suffer rape.

We can draw the conclusion that Peter Plogojowitz was the first person in his village to catch a genuine case of vampirism and, by infecting others with it, made a place for himself in history.

We can use this first example then to begin our list of genuine vampiric "qualities"—

1. The power to create a kind of epidemic of blood lust among chosen individuals, both male and female.

2. Vampires appear "undead" in the grave: the skin is fresh and there is no evident *rigor mortis* [the temporary stiffness of muscles occurring after death]; fresh blood still flows in their veins.

3. There appears to be evidence that the vampire also retains a strong sexual appetite and that this vigor exists even in the grave. . . .

Such an account could more easily have been written within the pages of a work of horror fiction. But this and many more such reports, signed and witnessed by local and even city officials and doctors, have formed the very real basis for beliefs in vampirism. These events, even though well-hidden within the yellowing pages of history books, are true as far as any historic event can be proven. They also created a very real and horrific fascination for the cultured ear of the romantic spirit that pervaded Europe at the time. It is easy to imagine the speculation, the elaboration, the transformation of such truths and their catalytic effect on audiences eager to shiver with fear at monstrous creatures who daunted far-away lands.

Eyewitness Accounts of Vampires

Montague Summers

Montague Summers was an ordained deacon who wrote prolifically on topics related to the occult, witchcraft, and supernatural phenomena. In his book *The Vampire in Europe*, from which the following article is excerpted, Summers presents an exhaustive amount of research into the eyewitness accounts of vampires, from early history through the late 1920s, when his book was first published. He collected oral and written narratives of vampire sightings and interactions not only from eyewitnesses themselves, but from relatives and acquaintances of those eyewitnesses. In his effort to present a thorough cataloging of vampire sightings in Europe over several centuries, Summers also refers to reputable published collections of eyewitness narratives. Summers was convinced that vampires exist in our world. Although the reader must ultimately decide this for himself, Summers' beliefs and the evidence he presents make a strong case that the reader cannot lightly dismiss.

Montague Summers, *The Vampire in Europe: True Tales of the Undead*. New York: Gramercy Books, 1996. Copyright © 1996 by Random House Value Publishing, Inc. Reproduced by permission.

Hungary, it may not untruly be said, shares with Greece and Slovakia the reputation of being that particular region of the world which is most terribly infested by the Vampire and where he is seen at his ugliest and worst. Nor is this common reputation undeserved. It was owing to a number of extraordinary and terrible occurences towards the end of the seventeenth century, which visitations persisted into the earlier years of the eighteenth century, that general attention was drawn to the problem of the Vampire, that theologians and students of the occult began to collect data of these happenings which made sufficient noise to be reported. . . .

The following incidents which happened about the year 1720 are placed beyond all manner of doubt both on account of the number and the position of the witnesses as also on account of the weight of the evidence which is sensible, circumstantial and complete. A soldier, who was billeted at the house of a farmer residing at Haidam, a village on the frontiers of Hungary, when one day he was at table with his host, the master of the house and the family, saw a stranger enter and take his place at the board among them. There seemed nothing extraordinary in this circumstance, but the goodman exhibited symptoms of unusual terror, as indeed did the rest of the company. Although he did not know what to think of it the soldier refrained from any comment, although it was impossible that he should not have remarked their confusion and fear. On the next morning the farmer was discovered dead in his bed, and then the reason for their perturbation could no longer be kept secret. They informed the soldier that the mysterious stranger was the farmer's old father, who had been dead and buried for more than ten years, and who had thus come and taken his place by the side of his son to forewarn him of his death, which indeed the terrible visitant had actually caused.

A Soldier's Sworn Testimony

As might have been expected, the soldier recounted this extraordinary incident to his friends and companions and so it came to the ears of several officers by whom it was carried to the general. A consultation was held, and it was resolved that the Count de Cadreras, commander of a corps of the Alandetti Infantry, should institute a full inquiry into so extraordinary circumstances. Accordingly this gentleman with several other officers, an army surgeon and a notary, paid an official visit to Haidam. Here they took the sworn depositions of all the people belonging to the house, and these without exception gave it on oath that the mysterious stranger was the father of the late master of the house, and that all the soldier had said and reported was the exact truth. These statements were unanimously corroborated by all the persons who lived in that district.

The Vampire Hunters Take Action

In consequence of this the officers decided that the body must be exhumed, and although ten years had passed it was found lying like a man who had just died, or even rather, like one who was in a heavy slumber, since when a vein was pierced the warm blood flowed freely as if that of a living person. The Count de Cadreras gave orders that the head should be completely severed, and then the corpse was once more laid in his grave. During their inquiry they also received information of many others who returned from the tomb, and among the rest of a man who had died more than thirty years before, who had come back no less than three times to his house at the hour of the evening's meal; and that on each occasion he had suddenly sprung upon an individual whose neck he bit fiercely, sucking the blood, and then vanishing with indescribable celerity. The first time he thus attacked his own brother, the second time one of his sons, and the third time one of the servants of the farm, so that all three expired instantly upon the spot. When this had been attested upon oath the Commissioner ordered that this man also should be disinterred, and he was found exactly like the first, just as a person who was still alive, the blood gushing out slab and red when an incision was made in the flesh. Orders were given that a great two-penny nail should be driven through the temples, and that afterwards the body should be laid again in the grave.

A third, who had been buried more than sixteen years, and who had caused the death of two of his sons by sucking their blood, was considered especially dangerous and forthwith cremated. The Commissioner made his report to the highest army tribunal, and they were so struck by the narration that they required him personally to deliver it to the Emperor Charles VI, who was so concerned at these extraordinary facts that he ordered a number of eminent lawyers, officers of the highest rank, the most skilled surgeons and physicians, and his most learned theologians to visit the district and conduct a most searching inquiry into the causes of these unusual and terrible occurences. The papers dealing with the case are still extant and the whole story was related in 1730 by the Count de Cadreras himself to a responsible official of the University of Fribourg who took down the details from the Count's own lips. It is hard to see how more reliable evidence is to be obtained of any happening or event.

It is no matter for surprise that in so sad and sick a country as Russia the tradition of the vampire should assume, if it be possible, an even intenser darkness. We find, indeed, a note of something deformed, as it were, something cariously diseased and unclean, a rank wealth of grotesque and fetid details which but serve to intensify the loathliness and horror. . . .

Passing from folk-tales, which none the less contain more than a grain or two of truth, we enter the realms of fact. In that famous work *Isis Unveiled* by Madame Blavatsky the following account is given of a Russian vampire, and it is stated that the details were told by an eyewitness of these terrible happenings.

An Eyewitness Speaks

"About the beginning of the present century, there occurred in Russia, one of the most frightful cases of Vampirism on record. The governor of the Province Tch— was a man of about sixty years, of a malicious, tyrannical, cruel, and jealous disposition. Clothed with despotic authority, he exercised it without stint, as his brutal instincts prompted. He fell in love with the pretty daughter of a subordinate official. Although the girl was betrothed to a young man whom she loved, the tyrant forced her father to consent to his having her marry him; and the poor victim, despite her despair, became his wife. His jealous disposition exhibited itself. He beat her, confined her to her room for weeks together, and prevented her seeing anyone except in his presence. He finally fell sick and died. Finding his end approaching, he made her swear never to marry again; and with fearful oaths threatened that, in case she did, he would return from his grave and kill her. He was buried in the cemetery across the river, and the young widow experienced no further annoyance, until, nature getting the better of her fears, she listened to the importunities of her former lover, and they were again betrothed.

On the night of the customary betrothal-feast, when all had returned, the old mansion was aroused by shrieks proceeding from her room. The doors were burst open and the unhappy woman was found lying on her bed in a swoon. At the same time a carriage was heard rumbling out of the courtyard. Her body was found to be black and blue in places, as from the effect of pinches, and from a slight puncture on her neck drops of blood were oozing. Upon recovering she stated that her deceased husband had suddenly entered her room, appearing exactly as in life, with the exception of a dreadful pallor; that he had upbraided her for her inconstancy, and then beaten and pinched her most cruelly. Her story was disbelieved; but the next morning the guard stationed at the other end of the bridge which spans the river, reported that, just before midnight, a black coach and six had driven furiously past them, towards the town, without answering their challenge.

The Vampire Proves His Power

The new governor, who disbelieved the story of the apparition, took nevertheless the precaution of doubling the guards across the bridge. The same thing happened, however, night after night; the soldiers declaring that the toll-bar at their station near the bridge would rise of itself, and the spectral equipage sweep by them despite their efforts to stop it. At the same time every night the coach would rumble into the courtyard of the house; the watchers, including the widow's family, and the servants, would be thrown into a heavy sleep, and every morning the young victim would be found bruised, bleeding and swooning as before. The town was thrown into consternation. The physicians had no explanation to offer; priests came to pass the night in prayer, but as midnight approached, all would be seized with the terrible lethargy. Finally, the archbishop of the province came, and performed the ceremony of exorcism in person, but the following morning the governor's widow was found worse than ever. She was now brought to death's door.

Protective Efforts Nearly Fail

The governor was now driven to take the severest measures to stop the ever-increasing panic in the town. He stationed fifty Cossacks along the bridge, with orders to stop the spectre-carriage at all hazards. Promptly at the usual hour, it was heard and seen approaching from the direction of the cemetery. The officer of the guard, and a priest bearing a crucifix, planted themselves in front of the toll-bar, and together shouted: 'In the name of God and the Czar, who goes there?' Out of the coach window was thrust a well-remembered head, and a familiar voice responded: 'The Privy Councillor of State and Governor C—!' At the same moment, the officer, the priest, and the soldiers were flung aside as by an electric shock, and the ghostly equippage passed by them, before they could recover breath.

The archbishop then resolved as a last expedient to resort to the time-honoured plan of exhuming the body, and pinning it to the earth with an oaken stake driven through its heart. This was done with great religious ceremony in the presence of the whole populace. The story is that the body was found gorged with blood, and with red cheeks and lips. At the instant that the first blow was struck upon the stake, a groan issued from the corpse, and a jet of blood spurted high in the air. The archbishop pronounced the usual exorcism, the body was re-interred, and from that time no more was heard of the Vampire."

Here we see that a strong individuality, cruelty and devilish hate are energized by the jealousy of lust—not love—and are perpetuated in this horrid manner even beyond the grave.

The following instance of vampirism was related to me by a friend who himself had it from Captain Pokrovsky in

1905. Captain Pokrovsky, a Russian-Lithuanian Guards officer, had been for a time relegated to his estates in Lithuania on account of some political indiscretion, but a little later he was allowed to spend a week or two with his uncle. His cousin, this nobleman's daughter, one morning invited him to go round with her while she was visiting her peasants. One man was pointed out to them as having mysteriously begun to fail in health and fade away since he had married his second wife. "He seems to shrivel from day to day, yet he is a rich farmer and eats meats ravenously at his meals." The man's sister, who lived with him, said, "Since he has re-married he cries out in the night." Captain Pokrovsky, who saw the man, described him as being pale and listless, not at all what a peasant of that stamp ought to appear, and accordingly he asked his cousin what actually was the matter with the fellow. The girl answered: "I do not know, but the villagers all declare that a vampire is getting at him."

The Doctor Is Called

The Captain was so interested in the case that he sent for a doctor who came from a considerable distance. The doctor after a careful examination reported that the man, whilst not anæmic in a medical sense, seemed to have lost a great deal of blood, but no wound could be found serious enough to account for such a drain. There was, however, a small puncture in the neck with inflamed edges, yet no swelling as might have been expected in the case of the bite of an insect. Tonics were promptly prescribed, and strengthening food was given to the invalid.

In due course Pokrovsky went back to his own home, but some time afterwards he inquired of his cousin concerning the anæmic peasant. She replied that in spite of the meat juice and red wine she had given him, the man had died, and that the wound in his neck at the time of death was far larger than when Pokrovsky had seen it. Further, the village was so entirely convinced that the man had been vampirized, that his wife, although she had frequently eaten heartily of food in public, had been seen to cross herself devoutly, and was a frequent attendant at Mass, immediately found it advisable, nay necessary, to leave the district. . . . Pokrovsky suggested that the woman may have played vampire subconsciously, whilst asleep; or that it may have been a case of vampiric possession. Either of these is possible, and it seems certain that one must be the correct explanation. Which of the two could only have been determined by an investigator upon the spot, an eye-witness. We have here then an indubitable [unquestionable] history of vampirism, an instance of very recent date.

Vampires in Europe

Anthony Masters

Anthony Masters was born in 1940 and educated at Kings College in Great Britain. He has worked as a novelist, journalist, researcher, and publisher. Masters's book, *The Natural History of the Vampire*, is the source for the following excerpt. The book has been studied and referred to by well-known scholars in the field of vampire studies. Masters introduces the reader to the famous historic vampires of Eastern and Western Europe: the Blood Countess, Elizabeth Bathory of Hungary; the infamous Gilles de Rais, the vampire who fought alongside Joan of Arc in France; Peter Kürten, the monster of Dusseldorf; and finally, Fritz Haarmann, whose vampire brain was donated to science. In recounting the infamous crimes of these real human vampires, Masters cites authentic documentation from court records, eyewitness accounts, newspaper headlines, and even testimony from the vampires themselves. This compelling evidence ultimately forces the reader to confront the chilling possibility that vampires do indeed live among us.

Anthony Masters, *The Natural History of the Vampire*. London: Rupert Hart Davis Ltd./Granada Publishing Ltd., 1972. Copyright © 1972 by Anthony Masters. Reproduced by permission of the literary estate of Anthony Masters.

Elizabeth of Bathory, the Blood Countess (Hungary, 1611)

Opinions vary as to how many young women were slaugh-tered by Countess Bathory. Some say three hundred—oth-ers claim it is more like six hundred. Sufficient to say that this psychotic middle-aged noblewoman, widow of the Count Nadasay, killed hundreds of young girls by draining them of their blood by various methods. One method, as documented by the court records of the time, was to 'put a terrified naked girl in a narrow iron cage furnished with pointed nails turned inward, hang it from the ceiling and sit beneath it enjoying the rain of blood that came down'. An-other little gimmick was

> an automat beautifully made by a German clock-smith, which was shaped like a girl and covered with red hair, and wearing red teeth torn from the mouth of some servant; the robot would clutch anyone that came near it in a tight em-brace and then transfix them with a series of sharp points that came out of her metal breasts. The blood ran down into a channel so that it could be collected, warmed over a fire and used for the Countess's bath.

. . . Bathory's psychotic mania was connected with her own beauty. She believed that the blood of virgins (or if not that, the blood of young women in general) would act as an excellent skin conditioner and she literally bathed in their blood. But

> on December 30th, 1610, Count Gyorsy Thurzo, her own cousin, the governor of the province, accompanied by sol-diers, gendarmes [police] and the village priest, raided the castle and arrested everybody in it. They had interrupted an orgy of blood. In the main hall of the castle they found one girl drained of blood and dead, another living girl whose body had been pierced with tiny holes, another who had just been tortured. In the dungeons and cellars they found and liberated a number of other girls, some of whose bod-ies had already been pierced and 'milked', others intact,

plump, well-fed, like well-kept cattle in their stalls. The dead bodies of some fifty more were subsequently exhumed.

The trial was held at Bitcse in 1611. The Countess refused to attend. Her servants were put to death and the Countess's life hung in the balance. Finally King Matthias II of Hungary commuted her sentence to life imprisonment, walled up in her own castle. . . .

Gilles de Rais (France, 1440)

He would contemplate those who had the most beautiful heads or members and have their bodies cruelly opened so that he might take delight in the sight of their internal organs; and, very often, when the said children died, he would sit on their stomachs and take pleasure in seeing them thus die and laugh at them . . . after which he had them burnt and converted into dust. (*Confessions of Gilles de Rais*, 1440)

De Rais's answer to his judges' questions about his deeds was 'that he had done them and perpetrated them following his own imagination and his own thought, without acting on anyone's advice and according to his own bent, purely for his own pleasure and carnal delectation and not for any other purpose or end.'

Gilles de Rais was in the amazing position of being both a national hero and an archetype villain. Around him he generated total insularity—which meant that the members of his court, rather like that of Elizabeth of Bathory, were heavily involved in their overlord's misdoings.

The Rise and Fall of a Hero

Gilles was immensely rich; he was both a scholar and a sportsman and had a high intellect. Owing to the death of his parents Gilles came under the influence of his grandfather, Jean de Craon, who was reputed to be unscrupulous and somewhat 'overpermissive.' Yet even de Craon confessed himself shocked by some of his grandson's later activities. The death of de Craon's own son at Agincourt made Gilles one of the wealthiest young men in France and his estates were doubled when he married Catherine de Thouers, a rich heiress. After joining the French court he quickly distinguished himself in action against the English and, in 1429, met Joan of Arc. Gilles fought beside Joan at Orleans and again at Patoy. Finally, when the Dauphin was crowned King of France at Rheims, it was Gilles' task to ride to the Abbey of Saint-Rémy to collect the sacred phial containing the unguent that had been the time-honoured anointment for the kings of France. When he was twenty-four Gilles was appointed a Marshal of France—an incredible feat at such a young age, even in those times.

But after Joan's death Gilles' terrible immaturity began to show itself. He became involved in local feuds, and stretched his own glory to [the] breaking point. Even his enormous fortune was unable to take the strain of financing both his court and army and gradually he began to go bankrupt.

Manoeuvred out of the political field, Gilles retired to his estates where he spent the last of his remaining millions in founding a chapel at Machecoul and equipping it with the full trappings of a cathedral, including a vast choir. In 1435 Gilles made a last public appearance before he retired into the dark shadows of his own self-indulgence. This last appearance was spectacular indeed; Gilles appeared in a full-scale pageant reenacting the siege and relief of the city of Orleans and the life and times of Joan of Arc. Then he disappeared—only to re-emerge at a later date on trial for his life.

From Hero to Monster

Raymond Rudorff writes in *Monsters:*

> From the moment he had retired, rumours began to circulate concerning the continual disappearances of young chil-

dren. In 1432, a twelve-year-old apprentice disappeared for ever from the village of Machecoul, after Gilles' cousin, Gilles de Sillé, had asked the boy's guardians for permission to send the lad on an errand. A nine-year-old boy tending cattle in the fields nearby vanished off the face of the earth after having been seen talking to de Sillé. A widow living in front of the castle complained of the disappearance of her eight-year-old son, 'a comely lad, white of skin and very capable'. Two weeks later, another boy missing and, after an outcry in the village, Gilles de Sillé came down from the castle and explained that the boys had been taken away as past ransom for his brother, who was being held prisoner by the English who were demanding a number of youths to be trained as pages.

Gilles spent five years committing the most incredible crimes of child murder and sodomy. Gilles also indulged in alchemy and sorcery—pursuits that were inextricably linked with the murder of hundreds of children. He kidnapped, raped and dismembered both young boys and girls. . . . After orgies involving massive blood-letting Gilles would retire to bed, seemingly in a state of coma—and would then return to the carnage with renewed ferocity. Finally, however, rumours grew to such proportions that the Church set up its own investigations, recoiling in horror at the furious necro-sadism of this warrior-prince-turned-vampire. He was arrested, tried and sentenced to death. At first Gilles desperately pleaded his innocence—and then, demonstrating his obvious schizophrenia, admitted everything, recounting in detail his perverted killings, blow by blow. At the same time Gilles clung desperately to his Christian faith, going to the gallows with an apparently peaceful mind.

What caused this young Marshal of France to change from a national hero to a monster is difficult to define. There is no doubt that he had led a violent life during which, in the cause of nationalism, he slaughtered hundreds. Perhaps Gilles found it impossible to give up shedding blood. . . .

Sergeant Bertrand (France, 1849)

The most direct case of 'live' vampirism known in France was the unfortunate case of Sergeant Bertrand who, at the time of his trial, was known throughout the country as 'The Vampire'. One July 10th, 1849, an investigation was held before a court-martial headed by Colonel Manselon. For months before, cemeteries in and around Paris has been broken into and the most appalling profanations had taken place, the graves desecrated and their contents strewn around the graveyard. The exhumed corpses were horribly mutilated.

> Every means were taken to discover the criminal; but the only result of the increased surveillance was that the scene of profanation was removed to the cemetery of Mont Parnasse, where the exhumations were carried to such an extent that the authorities were at their wit's ends. Considering, by the way, that all these cemeteries are surrounded by walls and have iron gates, which are kept closed, it certainly seems very strange that any ghoul or vampyre of solid flesh and blood should have been able to pursue his vocation so long undisturbed.

A trap was laid but the severely wounded vampire escaped, leaving behind him fragments of military clothing. Some soldiers of the 74th Regiment reported that one of their number had been admitted, severely wounded, to the military hospital shortly after midnight. The culprit was discovered. Bertrand was tried and sentenced to a year in prison. In his defence Bertrand stated that 'he would suddenly feel an irresistible need to destroy and mutilate corpses', after which he would fall into a coma.

In a letter written later from prison, Bertrand described his necrophilia in grotesquely matter-of-fact terms:

> If I have sometimes cut male corpses into pieces, it was only out of rage at not finding one of the female sex. Some nights I have had to dig up as many as a dozen men before finding a single woman in the common grave at Montparnasse.

Bertrand would open the corpse's stomach and embrace the corpse, and eventually he would destroy it.

Ornella Volta says of him:

> Bertrand did not recoil before obstacles: when he found an icy moat separating the cemetery of Douai from the city, he swam across it; if he stumbled over one of the man-traps that were set in certain cemeteries as a defense against would-be profaners, he did not let it worry him, but instead dismantled it and took it to pieces with all the aplomb of an expert, and if, during one of his habitual expeditions, he should hear people coming, he would lie perfectly still in the grave next to the corpse; when dogs belonging to the keeper of the cemetery came barking towards him he merely stared them in the eyes. His look must have had a hypnotic power because, like Dracula's, it made animals lower their eyes and tails and slink away in silence. . . .

Peter Kürten, the Monster of Dusseldorf (Germany, 1883–1931)

> The most extraordinary and horrible point about Kürten's nocturnal prowling lay in the association with the vampire and werewolf of ancient tradition. It was his habit, and his principal satisfaction to receive the stream of blood that gushed from his victim's wounds into his mouth. (M.S. Wagner, a journalist covering the Kürten case)

Peter Kürten was a very strange man indeed. Totally nondescript. He was a neat dresser, wore horn-rimmed glasses and had a minute moustache. Altogether he committed twenty-nine murders and assaults, causing Dusseldorf years of fear and giving it a reputation of horror that filtered throughout Europe. Kürten suffered from haematodipsia, basically a sexual thirst for blood. . . . His father was a near-alcoholic, his mother a homely woman whom Kürten thought a saint. Later in his life he was to marry a mother-figure—a woman who was forced to marry him as he repeatedly threatened her life. She never knew of her husband's crimes until the very end—when he confessed like a naughty child to her—

and it was she who went to the police and gave him up.

At the time of his trial Kürten wrote appalling letters to the parents of the young girls and children that he had slaughtered. 'What do you want, Madame? I need blood as others need alcohol,' wrote Kürten to the mother of one of his five-year-old victims. He spent years in prison, but mainly for burglary or theft, and he was not discovered to be the Dusseldorf monster until the end of his murderous career—and until an epileptic named Hans Strausberg had already been arrested in his place. . . .

In April 1931 Kürten was sentenced to death nine times over (in accordance with German law).

He did not appeal against his sentence and awaited execution with total calm.

Fritz Haarmann (Germany, 1879–1923)

The London *Daily Express* of April 17th, 1925, printed the following remarkable paragraph:

VAMPIRE BRAIN.
PLAN TO PRESERVE IT FOR SCIENCE.
Berlin, *Thursday, April 16th.*

The body of Fritz Haarmann, executed yesterday at Hanover for twenty-seven murders, will not be buried until it has been examined at Göttingen University.

Owing to the exceptional character of the crimes—most of Haarmann's victims were *bitten to death*—the case aroused tremendous interest among German scientists. It is probable that Haarmann's brain will be removed and preserved by the University authorities.—*Central News.*

Fritz Haarmann was nicknamed the Hanover Vampire. Born in 1879, Haarmann went through military school to the army, and on discharge was arrested for offences against children. As a result of the trial Haarmann was sent to an asylum as he was considered to be unbalanced. On release he returned home to Hanover, became involved in gigantic quarrels with his father, left again and rejoined a crack army unit. Here he served for a period, received excellent reports, was discharged and ran into trouble again through both violence and larceny. Haarmann was jailed several times and in 1918 he was released into a beaten Germany. He began a small cook-shop, hawked meat and made money on the side as a police informer. But Haarmann had one more activity—and a particularly fearsome one.

A Secret Life at Night

At night he would wander the halls of the main Hanover railway station and there pick up a variety of youngsters who were either refugees or had run away from one part or another of war-torn Germany. Haarmann won their confidence and invited them back home.

Initially Haarmann was arrested for having indecent relations with an eighteen-year-old runaway. He received nine months' imprisonment. Some years later, whilst Haarmann awaited trial for twenty-seven murders, he stated: 'At the time when the police arrested me the head of the boy Friedel Rothe was hidden under a newspaper behind the oven. Later on I threw it into the canal'.

A Partner in Crime

Haarmann had an accomplice to his carnage—Hans Grans, who met Haarmann in 1919. . . .

The *News of the World* of December 7th, 1924, had the following account of the Haarmann-Grans trial under the heading 'Vampires' Victims':

> The killing of altogether twenty-four young men is laid at his door, the horror of the deeds being magnified by the allegation that he sold to customers for consumption the flesh of those he did not himself eat. . . . With Haarmann in the dock appeared a younger man, his friend Hans Grans, first accused of assisting in the actual murders but now charged

with inciting him to commit them and with receiving stolen property. The police are still hunting for a third man, Charles, also a butcher, who is alleged to have completed the monstrous trio . . . the prosecuting attorney has an array of nearly 200 witnesses to prove that all the missing youths were done to death in the same horrible way. . . . He would take them to his rooms, and after a copious meal would praise the looks of his young guests. Then he would kill them after the fashion of a vampire. Their clothes he would put up on sale in his shop, and the bodies would be cut up and disposed of with the assistance of Charles. In open court, however, Haarmann admitted that Grans often used to select his victims for him. More than once, he alleged, Grans beat him for failing to kill the 'game' brought in, and Haarmann would keep the corpses in a cupboard until they could be got rid of, and one day the police were actually in his rooms when there was a body awaiting dismemberment. The back of the place abutted on the river, and the bones and skulls were thrown into the water. Some of them were discovered, but their origin was a mystery until a police inspector paid a surprise visit to the prisoner's home to inquire into a dispute between Haarmann and an intended victim who escaped.

Evidence Condemns Grans and Haarmann

Another *News of the World* account on December 21st [1924] states:

> The details of the atrocious crimes for which Haarmann will shortly pay with his life were extremely revolting. All his victims were between 12 and 18 years of age, and it was proved that the accused actually sold the flesh for human consumption. He once made sausages in his kitchen, and, together with the purchaser, cooked and ate them. . . . Some alienists hold that even then the twenty-four murders cannot possibly exhaust the full toll of Haarmann's atrocious crimes, and estimate the total as high as fifty. With the exception of a few counts, the prisoner made minutely detailed confessions and for days the court listened to his grim narrative of how he cut up the bodies of his victims and disposed of the fragments in various ways. He consistently repudiated the imputation of insanity, but at the same time

maintained unhesitatingly that all the murders were committed when he was in a state of trance, and unaware of
what he was doing. This contention was specifically brushed
aside by the Bench, which in its judgment pointed out that
according to his own account of what happened, it was necessary for him to hold down his victims by hand in a peculiar way before it was possible for him to inflict a fatal bite
on their throats. Such action often necessarily involved
some degree of deliberation and conscious purpose.

Skulls and bones found in the river during the months of
May, June, and July 1924, together with an open confrontation with a boy who accused him of indecency, put the finger of suspicion on Haarmann. There is no doubt that Haarmann's behaviour was vampire-like, particularly as he bit at
the throats of his victims. He was executed in 1923 whilst
Grans received twelve years' imprisonment. In 1924, the
newspapers recorded that six hundred people had disappeared in Hanover. Of these many were boys between 14
and 18—and a good proportion of these may well have
been butchered by Haarmann and Grans.

Modern American Vampires

Norine Dresser

Norine Dresser is a folklorist in the department of English at California State University, Los Angeles, and a research associate at the Center for the Study of Comparative Folklore and Mythology at UCLA. Dresser had never really thought much about the image of the vampire until she was mistakenly assumed to be a vampire expert based on comments she made in a media interview. As Dresser recalls in her introduction to *American Vampires*, this misunderstanding "plunged [her] into an investigation of vampires and they began to invade [her] life." In this excerpt from *American Vampires*, Dresser introduces the reader to several individuals who identify themselves as vampires and regularly either drink blood or feed on the emotional energy of other human beings. Dresser interviews and observes the vampires, and others who know them, in an attempt to piece together an image of their lives, their rituals, and their hunger for human blood or energy. According to Dresser, these

"American vampires" demonstrate "the power and vitality of the vampire symbol in this country."

Melody remembers that she was wearing a low-cut, hot-pink dress the first time she met Pam, the vampire. It was 1985 and Melody's friend Brad had arranged the meeting. "Pam's always looking for someone else. Would you be interested?"

The modest apartment filled with books and plants was located in an East Coast city and seemed almost secluded because of the quiet created by the well-insulated building. Four young people—Melody, twenty-five; the others in their early thirties—had gathered to participate in a practice they were not ashamed of, but were nonetheless wary of divulging to others, as revealed by the clothespin holding closed the orange drapes. . . .

Pam stabbed one of Brad's fingers with a sterilized hypodermic needle of a type normally used for animals. She pierced the skin, squeezed the finger, squeezed some more; then she sucked from it. When she finished one finger, she repeated the steps with the next one, licking each finger when she was finished. . . .

After spending about twenty minutes stabbing Brad's fingers and then sucking them, Pam turned to Melody and said, "Okay, you're next."

Thus began Melody's initiation into the act of vampirism, playing the role of donor for Pam's belief in her need for fresh, warm human blood.

Ordinary People, Unusual Lifestyle

The activities just described were freely and enthusiastically reported because Pam, Melody, and Brad have a curiosity about their own behavior. Admittedly, these young people are not representative of a large population. They are but a minute fraction of modern society. Their behavior is carried out in private, of their own volition, to the harm of no one, and for the purpose of satisfying certain inner needs, sometimes understood, other times not. In spite of the reality that they are imitating behavior not publicly sanctioned, they do not think of themselves as aberrant.

If you were to meet them they would not strike you as being strange in any way. They seem like ordinary people functioning positively in the external world with family commitments and responsible jobs. One of them is employed full time in the art world. Another holds a government position requiring knowledge of the sciences and well-developed problem-solving abilities. The third works in the medical field. . . .

What follows is a documentation of ways in which Americans identify with and imitate the vampire's behavior. The intention is to understand the vampires' place in our culture and to examine their impact on the lives of ordinary people.

The Life of a Donor

After her first experience at being a donor, Melody became a regular visitor to Pam for this purpose, sometimes seeing her once a month or going as often as once a week. "I do it for my own personal enjoyment. I mean, I have a very close and enjoyable friendship with Pam. Even if we didn't have this kind of relationship, I'd still be friends with her, so I think this just brings us closer." Melody and Pam have maintained this association for over three years.

Melody has never concerned herself with wondering if there was anything physically real about Pam's being a vampire. "It's not for me to say. If Pam drinks blood and she says she's a vampire, who am I to say she's not? I don't have any

evidence that says she's not. I don't know any other re-
quirements for being a vampire, except if you drink blood,
and she does."

However, Melody rejects the vampire label for herself, and
has never been a donor to anyone else. She has further discovered that it is wise not to let any boyfriends know about
her activities with Pam. Melody learned this the hard way. On
several occasions in the past she thought she would be hon-
est with the men she was romantically involved with and let
them know about her relationship with Pam. "I just kind of
mentioned it. I mean, I didn't mention any names, but it
kind of scared a couple of them off." As a result, Melody now
keeps her donor life a secret from potential suitors. . . .

Meet the Vampires

Pam's own vampiric practices became fixed five years ago
when she encountered Kristin, who lives in another state.
Kristin claims her need for blood to be one cup per week
during winter and three-quarters to one and one-quarter
pint per week during the summer. She doesn't get "high" on
blood. Rather, it makes her feel energized, full of life, satisfied. Animal blood doesn't supply what she needs. She says
that without warm human blood she becomes weakened or
sick. Once she even ended up in the hospital needing a
transfusion.

Kristin, also in her thirties, stated that she obtains blood
from donors rather than victims, whom she describes as
"Those who are forced to give." On the other hand, donors
give willingly with or without an exchange of something,
that is, sex, money, dinner. To find donors she usually
avoids bars and picking up people. Instead, her friends find
other friends, or she meets them at places such as bowling
alleys, arcades, or occasionally in a library or at a park.

At times it is difficult to find donors. When the "hunger

gets bad," she starts pacing. Sometimes she has to go to another town to find donors. "Explaining to someone of my need happens when the time is right. I sense it." She starts out talking about movies, then the occult, and from there she broaches the subject. "There have been times at the last minute people back out. I let them go. All is done willingly and with agreement not to tell.". . .

A Vampire Gene?

Kristin perceives of herself as having been born that way. She says that vampirism ran in her family, with only one or two per generation. She claims that as an infant she kept biting herself until she bled. When she was growing up, other schoolchildren teased her about her pallor. Bright sunlight hurt her eyes, and today she must wear sunglasses during the daylight. Although she has inherited her condition, she believes she can pass it on to others through her bite and transmission of something she refers to as a "V" cell. She "transfuses" varying "dosages" of the "V" cell to different donors. Feedings take place day or night, but she prefers darkness and must be alone with the donor. . . .

It was through Kristin that Pam believes she received the "V" cell, transmitted when Pam was initiated into the donor role for Kristin. This subsequently created Pam's need for donors, which began to manifest itself during a full moon about six months after Pam had first given blood to Kristin.

Pam describes physical changes she believes have taken place in her as a result of this "V" cell transfusion—a kind of itching and throbbing in the gums above her canine teeth, especially during the full and new moons when she has a craving. Pam says that hot weather increases the hunger. "It feels like little pinch-like sensations or a bite or a burning sort of feeling in the veins." Kristin, too, reports the same type of sensations, describing her veins as feeling like they are on fire during hot weather. . . .

Pam doesn't quite understand the changes going on within her. She reports that ever since she has been giving and taking human blood she has stopped being plagued by canker sores. She doesn't comprehend why. In addition, she wonders whether or not her condition would ever be passed on to her child, if she were to have one. . . .

Since Pam has only been drinking human blood for a few years, she believes she could stop the habit, if necessary. However, at present she finds the feeding so emotionally and physically satisfying that she has no desire to discontinue the practice. She says that a few hours following a feeding her symptoms of need stop—her eyes become normal, and she sleeps well. It has a calming effect on her.

Here are two women who appear to take pleasure—even pride—in the act of vampirism and in calling themselves vampires. Neither of them seems to have any qualms about being associated with a creature who in the past was reviled. They seem not to be dealing with the notion that they will live forever, but rather to be applying the vampire name to themselves based primarily on their habits of drinking blood. There is no association whatsoever with the undead state—not being able to rest in peace—usually associated with vampires. . . .

The Order of the Vampyre

There is another group of persons who identify with the vampire in a different way, who think of themselves as outside the schema of contemporary vampire phenomena. These are members of the Order of the Vampyre, a special-interest division within the Temple of Set, which evolved from the closing of Anton Szandor LaVey's Church of Satan. . . .

LaVey's goal was to encourage the study of the black arts

and repudiate what he saw as the religious hypocrisy of conventional society. However, LaVey's church closed in 1975 when many of its members resigned to form a new organization, the Temple of Set.

Setians value both individualism and self-actualization. For those who have risen to qualify for the Order of the Vampyre (OV), their goal is to become acquainted with the characteristics of the Vampyric Being. They do not use blood in any manner, nor do they identify with the undead state. Instead they look at some of the alleged powers of the vampire creature, seeking the essence behind the myth, the noble quality of the archetype—elegance, sophistication, and charm. . . .

Working to Improve the Image of the Vampire

Recognizing that the real Vampyre can be hideous, the OV acknowledges that it can be glamourous as well and encourages learning the skill of applying cosmetics, using their voices effectively, and acquiring methods of holding another person's gaze. One of their co-Grand Masters is Lilith Aquino (no relation to the president of the Philippines). Her attractive appearance—red dress contrasting with well-made-up fair complexion and striking black hair—during an interview on the *Oprah Winfrey* television show gave testimony to the skillfulness she has acquired, serving well as a role model for other members of the OV.

Development of the powers of imagination, visualization, and invisibility is encouraged in this order along with the use and study of art, music, and literature. It is clear that despite their name, these Vampyres have a different agenda from the other vampires already described. Perhaps that is one of the reasons they have chosen to spell their name differently, which also helps to maintain their sense of mystery. . . .

Ironically, the Temple of Set deplores other kinds of vampires, called psychic vampires. This idea is based upon a passage found in Anton LaVey's *The Satanic Bible*, which describes psychic vampires as persons who make you feel guilty if you don't do favors for them—those who, like leeches, drain others of their energy and emotions. . . .

The Temple of Set is currently headed by Lilith's husband, Michael A. Aquino, Ph.D., a controversial figure by virtue of his unusual looks—inverted V-shaped eyebrows, Friar Tuck hairdo, round face, and dark robe garb—and his occupation. He is a Vietnam War–decorated lieutenant colonel in the U.S. Army, now on active reserve, working in military intelligence as a psychological warfare officer, and holding security clearance for top-secret information. . . .

Beliefs in vampires as real entities might seem anachronistic in today's high-tech and scientifically aware society, but, surprisingly, there are pockets of belief in this unreal creature.

Psychic Vampires

Joe H. Slate

Joe H. Slate is a practicing psychologist in Alabama. He has extensive experience researching topics centered on altered states of consciousness and psychic phenomena. In this excerpt from his book, *Psychic Vampires*, Slate presents his research on the human energy system, which he argues "energize[s] and sustain[s] our existence." Psychic vampirism is a serious threat to the ability of the human energy system to successfully promote growth and potential in our lives. The psychic vampire is typically "deficient in energy resources," resulting in the need to psychically feed off the "energy reserve of a host victim." Slate explains the ways in which psychic vampirism occurs and provides answers to many of the questions readers might have about this unusual type of vampire. The specialized evidence Slate presents is particularly significant because it urges a revision of the common definition of the vampire to include beings who can perhaps still be considered vampiric even though they do not feed off the blood of others. This knowledge forces the reader to, at the very least, confront his or her own preconceived notions of what a vampire is or is not in an attempt to determine whether they do in fact exist.

Psychic vampirism is a widespread yet often unrecognized human energy phenomenon that can interrupt our growth and impede our progress. . . . [I]t exists in a variety of forms, each of which subtly consumes its victim's energy and over the long haul, erodes the energy system itself. Although no known force can totally destroy the human energy system because of its cosmic makeup, psychic vampirism can impair its functions and seriously damage its capacity to energize growth. Consequently, understanding psychic vampirism . . . [is] critical in our struggle to realize our growth potentials and achieve our highest level of self-fulfillment.

Although psychic vampirism exists in various forms, the expression, unless qualified, typically denotes psychic vampirism between two persons, the one being the psychic vampire and the other the host victim. In that context, the psychic vampire, who is deficient in energy resources, taps the energy reserve of a host victim for the express purpose of extracting energy from it. The immediate effects vary but usually include a new surge of revitalizing energy for the psychic vampire and a critical depletion of essential energy for the vampirized victim.

Unfortunately, the long-term consequences of recurring vampire assaults on the energy system can be extremely harmful, not only for the host victim but for the psychic vampire as well. Short-circuiting the internal energy system sabotages the psychic vampire's personal development, thus arresting healthy development and making repeated vampire interactions necessary. The host victim's energy system, on the other hand, becomes stressed by the depletion of energy and overworked in order to generate new energy. Given recurrent attacks, the victim's energy supply can become chronically depleted and the internal energy system itself can become severely damaged. . . .

Explaining Psychic Vampirism

Like most human behaviors, psychic vampirism can be explained from a variety of perspectives, each of which can help us to better understand this complex phenomenon. While the perspectives that follow focus primarily on psychic vampirism between two persons, they have implications for other forms as well.

One rather simplistic view holds that psychic vampirism is basically instinctual, a built-in component of a larger drive to survive. As such, it is essentially beyond our control—all efforts to alter or extinguish it are, for the most part, futile. This pessimistic view fails to note, however, that psychic vampirism, unlike instincts, usually develops gradually, thus offering ample opportunity for corrective intervention anywhere along the way.

Another view of psychic vampirism holds that we are first and foremost biological beings who are driven by certain basic physical drives—hunger, thirst, sex, sleep, activity, comfort, and energy. Here, psychic vampirism is explained simply as a means to an end—it's a way of satisfying the human need for energy. Individual differences, past experiences, and unique personal characteristics are seen as relatively unimportant. A major contribution of this perspective is its recognition of energy as a basic human drive; its major limitation is a failure to recognize the critical importance of responsible choice and self-determination in satisfying that drive.

Another view of psychic vampirism is based on the concept that seeking pleasure while avoiding pain is the major motivational force underlying human behavior. From this perspective, psychic vampirism is a raw, untamed drive that demands instant pleasure and gratification. It is easier and more pleasurable to tap the energy supply of another person than to develop one's own energy system. This limited perspective opens the floodgates for psychic vampirism to develop as a controlling force in our lives. Like the other perspectives discussed, it minimizes our capacity to take command of our personal growth and shape our own destiny.

The Limitations of Various Perspectives

Psychic vampirism also focuses on the social nature of our makeup. In this perspective, we interact with individuals and groups that are consistent with our roles and needs as social beings. Typically, when we give something to the relationship we expect to gain something in return. Ideally, social interactions are mutually satisfying with everyone getting a fair return; however, the investments and rewards of many human relationships are unequal. In psychic vampirism, the interaction is reduced to a calculated, unbalanced encounter in which the vampire benefits and the victim loses. A limitation of this perspective is its tendency to minimize the importance of influences beyond the social situation, including individual differences in values, predispositions, and interests.

Another perspective of psychic vampirism emphasizes perception as the major determinant of human behavior, and that psychic vampires are victims of their own perceptions. They engage in vampire behaviors because of the way they see themselves and the situation—they behave in ways that make sense to them based on their perceptions. They, in fact, see no other alternative. A serious flaw in this is its tendency to reject our capacity to evaluate situations, make responsible choices, determine outcomes, and eventually change the ways we see ourselves and the conditions around us.

An extremely narrow yet popular belief of psychic vampirism explains the phenomenon as basically an issue of good versus evil. It says psychic vampirism is more than an energy phenomenon—it is an encounter between the vampire bent on evil and the unsuspecting, innocent victim. Driven by dark, malicious forces, the psychic vampire seeks not only energy but domination and, in some instances, even destruction of the unsuspecting victim. Combating vampirism focuses on repulsing and defeating the vampire, who is then forced to find an unwitting victim elsewhere, a strategy that unfortunately perpetuates the vampire cycle. By focusing on morality issues only, this simplistic belief overlooks the developmental nature and complex functions of the human energy system. For the victim, it prescribes procedures that hold little relevance for long-term growth and personal empowerment. . . .

Defining the Psychic Vampire

Historically, our concept of psychic vampirism has been limited, and the extent of psychic vampirism throughout the world has been grossly underestimated. We now know that psychic vampirism is not only widespread; it also exists in many forms. . . . Taken together, contemporary psychic vampirism can be grouped into three major categories:

1. *One-on-one Psychic Vampirism.* This category includes any form of psychic vampirism between two persons, the one being the psychic vampire and the other the host victim. In the typical one-on-one vampire encounter, the psychic vampire taps into the energy system of the host victim for the express purpose of extracting energy. The vampire episode can be consensual or nonconsensual as well as deliberate or spontaneous. Whatever the nature of the vampire encounter, the results are the same—an instant but transient surge of energy for the vampire, and a critical loss of energy

for the vampirized victim. Unfortunately, the psychic vampire's energy needs are satisfied only temporarily, thus necessitating repeated attacks. For the host victim of recurrent attacks, the long-term consequences can be extremely harmful.

2. *Group Psychic Vampirism.* This category, which we could call collective vampirism, includes any form of vampirism that involves groups, organizations, or institutions. In its most insidious and destructive form, it can involve the organized vampire efforts of large numbers of persons. Power, wealth, and control are among the major goals of group vampirism. Its wide-ranging symptoms can include criminal activity, environmental pollution, irresponsible exploitation of the earth's natural resources, and flagrant abuse of human rights. When sufficiently widespread and culturally ingrained, group psychic vampirism can be so powerful that it affects global conditions with consequences that can span centuries.

3. *Parasitic Vampirism.* In sharp contrast to other forms of psychic vampirism, parasitic vampirism is an internal form of psychic vampirism turned against the self. Tragically, parasitic vampires are twice the victim—they are both vampire and host victim. They are driven by self-destructive mechanisms that are like bloodsucking vampires with a demonic appetite—the more they devour, the more they demand. The effects of parasitic vampirism are relentlessly self-constricting and self-disempowering. By attacking from the inside, parasitic vampirism drains its host of essential energy and weakens the ability to cope, even with minor stress. In the long run, parasitic vampirism grinds down the self's energy system and seriously impairs its capacity to generate new energy. . . .

Common Questions About Psychic Vampires

1. How do psychic vampires differ from folklore or fictional vampires?

In contrast to folklore and fictional vampirism, psychic vampires feed on energy rather than blood, and they possess no supernatural powers. Deficient in energy, and with their energy system usually impaired, they seek other energy options. Contrary to prevailing stereotypes, typical psychic vampires are not agents of evil bent on the destruction of their victims. Although certain fringe "vampire groups" are known to practice various folklore vampire rituals, they have demonstrated none of the supernatural powers attributed to folklore vampires. . . .

2. What causes psychic vampirism?

Although the causes vary (depending on the form of psychic vampirism), they usually include a combination of developmental and situational factors. For one-on-one as well as parasitic vampirism, early childhood experiences, including parent-child relationships, are especially critical. Children who are either pampered or who have a cold, distant relationship with either parent seem to be particularly prone to psychic vampirism. Also, certain personality characteristics such as identity conflict, a poor self-image, and deep-seated insecurity and inferiority are common among psychic vampires of both sexes. Psychic vampirism can be precipitated by situational factors such as severely traumatic events, occupational problems, and family crises, to mention only a few of the possibilities. On a large scale, group psychic vampirism is often associated with corrupt motives and sweeping misuse of power and influence.

3. Is psychic vampirism a recent phenomenon?

Evidence suggests that psychic vampirism long predated folklore and fictional versions of vampirism. The history of civilization is replete with instances of psychic vampirism in its various forms.

4. How dangerous is a single psychic vampire attack?

The typical psychic vampire episode is an energy phenomenon in which the vampire is infused with a fresh supply of energy at the expense of the victim donor. While the loss of energy for the donor can be minimal or barely noticeable, even a single vampire attack can have serious consequences, depending on the conditions of the attack as well as the mental and physical states of the host victim. . . .

5. What are the effects of repeated psychic vampire attacks on the victim?

For the victim of recurrent psychic vampire attacks, the typical effects are a significant loss of energy and, in the long run, damage to the internal energy system itself. Other common effects are chronic fatigue, difficulty concentrating, sleep disturbances, irritability, lowered tolerance for frustration, depressed mood, excessive anxiety, sexual indifference, and impaired memory. Extreme, long-term exposure to psychic vampirism can result in biological wear-and-tear accompanied by an array of physical symptoms, including a compromised immune system and even life-threatening illness. There is some evidence to suggest that certain chronic respiratory problems and gastrointestinal disturbances are associated with recurrent psychic vampire attacks.

6. What are the long-term effects of psychic vampirism on the vampire?

Over time, the psychic vampire drive can become so powerful that it dominates the person's life. Eventually, virtually every aspect of the vampire's life centers around meeting critical energy needs. Unfortunately, as the vampire drive becomes stronger, the vampire's inner energy mechanisms slowly deteriorate like muscles that are never used. The vampire's inner energy system can become so fragile that it is finally short-circuited and rendered totally nonfunctional. Like an essential body organ that no longer functions, the incapacitated energy system requires external life support. In the case of psychic vampirism, that life support is the energy system of a host victim.

7. Can psychic vampires strike from a distance?

Vampire attacks can occur during physical contact—such as a handshake or touch on the shoulder—or they can occur at distances of up to many miles. Vampire assaults involving great distances, however, are associated only with advanced psychic vampirism. They usually occur in the context of an ongoing association or relationship, though not necessarily of the romantic kind. . . .

8. What are the attack strategies used by psychic vampires?

The attack strategies used by psychic vampires vary, depending on the type of vampirism and the surrounding conditions. The deliberate vampire attack typically consists of (1) a focused mental state in which the host victim is the object of attention, (2) a strong intent to tap the energy system of the victim, and (3) forcefully taking energy from the victim. Interviews with experienced psychic vampires found that imagery of an energy channel connecting them to their host victim throughout the attack is common. In the spontaneous attack, the strategies are similar but effortless and at times, unconscious. Often underlying the psychic vampire attack are certain hidden motives, such as domination, punishment, and control. The energizing effects of subduing others and forcefully taking energy from them are often secondary to the rewards of the conquest itself. . . .

9. Is there any hope for the psychic vampire?

For the vampire, the recovery process must include a recognition of the disempowering nature of psychic vampirism on both vampire and victim, a firm resolve to develop a more functional internal energy system, and, finally, mastery of relevant recovery strategies.

Unfortunately, the popular notions of evil associated with psychic vampirism contribute to the vampire's tendency toward self-rejection and complicates any recovery effort. At the same time, attributing evil to psychic vampirism handicaps the potential victim's efforts to acquire effective vampire protection and coping skills. Also, the "vampire" label itself can encourage rejection of the psychic vampire who is too often seen as a depraved, deviant creature to be avoided at all costs. Such exaggerated stereotyping can actually increase our vulnerability to psychic vampirism. It is possible to become so vampire phobic in our perception of psychic vampirism as an evil threat that fear alone consumes enormous amounts of our energy, thus actually exhausting our defense and coping resources. The energy wasted on false perceptions and exaggerated fear could be put to much better use, such as energizing our personal development and perhaps helping others.

Chapter 2

Fact or Fiction?

The Facts Beyond
the Fiction:
Arguments
Against the
Existence of
Vampires

Eyewitness Accounts of Vampires Can Be Explained

Daniel Farson

Daniel Farson is exceptionally qualified to write on the subject of vampires. Not only is he the author of *The Man Who Wrote Dracula*, the most authoritative and well-known biography on Bram Stoker, but Farson is also Stoker's great-nephew. In the following article, excerpted from another of his books on vampires and the supernatural, Farson offers rational explanations for the eyewitness accounts of vampire activity recorded in many cultures throughout history. Discussing the historical context within which these eyewitness accounts have been reported, he provides scientific, medical, and psychological evidence that work to explain that the "vampires" people believe they saw were really the result of bodies affected by natural decomposition processes, accidental premature burial, and superstitious imaginings created by the human unconscious. Farson never directly states that vampires do not exist. Instead, the reader is presented

Daniel Farson, *The Supernatural: Vampires, Zombies, and Monster Men*. London: Aldus Books Ltd., 1975. Copyright © 1975 by Aldus Books Ltd. Reproduced by permission.

with a body of evidence that, even while it seems designed to prove that vampires do not exist, succeeds in leaving the question open for the reader to ponder.

"Bring out your dead!" That cry was horrifyingly familiar to the people who lived in times of plague. Carts piled high with corpses would trundle by night after night, bound for the burial pit. A red cross marked the doors of the stricken, and the sick were often abandoned even by their own family for fear of contagion. Streets became blocked with decomposing bodies as the living left the towns to the dead and dying. It is easy to understand how terrified people must have been by this devastating disease that flared up periodically in Europe from ancient times right down to the 18th century. Never knowing where it might strike or when it might end must have made the plague more alarming even than warfare. Such an epidemic would leave an area depressed mentally as well as physically, creating the ideal climate for panic.

The worst plague of all was the Black Death which swept through Europe in the 14th century. It claimed millions of victims—a quarter of Europe's population. When the Black Death finally began to subside, a strange delusion took possession of whole communities in the region that is now Germany. It was known as the Dance of St. Vitus, and the nervous disorder that is marked by jerky involuntary movements is still known by that name today. The dancers seemed to lose their senses, performing wild leaps, screaming, and foaming at the mouth. Regardless of the dismayed crowds that watched them, they danced together for hours in this strange state of delirium until they fell from sheer fatigue. They saw nothing and heard nothing except for some who were haunted by religious visions. In spite of this, the priests believed that the dancers were possessed by the devil, and tried to pacify them by exorcism. . . .

This frenzied dancing seems to have been a form of collective hysteria—a result of the nervous strain left by the Black Death. In the same kind of hysteria, rumors of vampirism would be especially likely to spread in times of pestilence, and would grow in the retelling. Another explanation for stories of vampires is even more convincing: the high frequency in those days of premature burial or of accidental burial alive. This was all the more probable in times of plague when people were terrified of infection, and disposed of bodies as hastily as possible.

Premature Burial and the Belief in Vampires

Strangely enough it has always been difficult to ascertain exactly when death occurs. Far from being rare, premature burial happened frequently in the past, and similar accidents can still happen today. As recently as 1974 doctors in a British hospital were dissecting a body for a kidney transplant when they realized to their horror that the corpse was breathing. This is not an isolated case. Recently in a southern state of America, an unmarried mother-to-be became so agitated at the sight of a policeman knocking on her door that she collapsed, and was certified as dead. A week after her burial, her mother arrived and insisted on seeing the body for herself. When the grave was opened it was discovered that the baby had been born, and that the mother's fingers had been worn down in the effort to scratch her way out of the coffin.

If we can make such mistakes today with all our medical knowledge imagine how easy errors must have been in the days when such states as catalepsy (a trancelike condition which might last for several weeks), epilepsy, or apparent death from suffocation or poison were not properly recognized. . . .

Even those who were simply in a drunken stupor might have awakened to find themselves interred forever in the darkness. It is hard to imagine a more appalling fate: first the gradual realization of what had happened, then the panicky and hopeless attempts to get out, and finally the slow suffocation. If the grave of someone prematurely buried was broken into by body snatchers seeking a body for dissection or by robbers hoping to find a valuable ring on one of the fingers, it would be discovered that the body had twisted into a different position in the cramped space. The searchers would probably find also that the shroud was torn and bloody, that there was blood on the fingers and nails from the wretched person's efforts to claw a way out, and that the mouth was bloody from being bitten in the final agony. How easily these signs could be attributed to vampirism.

Dr. Herbert Mayo, Professor of Anatomy at King's College, London, realized this truth in 1851 and wrote: "That the bodies, which were found in the so called Vampyr state, instead of being in a new or mystical condition, were simply alive in the common way, or had been so for some time subsequent to their interment; that, in short, they were the bodies of persons who had been buried alive, and whose life, where it yet lingered, was finally extinguished through the ignorance and barbarity of those who disinterred them." In other words, some alleged vampires might still have been alive when the stake was plunged through their heart. Dr. Mayo quoted the case of a man who was believed to have become a vampire, and who was exhumed. "When they opened his grave," Mayo says, ". . . his face was found with a color, and his features made natural sorts of movements, as if the dead man smiled. He even opened his mouth as if he would inhale fresh air. They held the crucifix before him, and called in a loud voice, 'See, this is Jesus Christ who redeemed your soul from hell, and died for you.' After the sound had acted on his organs of hearing, and he had connected perhaps some ideas with it, tears began to flow from the dead man's eyes. Finally, when after a short prayer for his poor soul, they proceeded to hack off his head, the corpse uttered a screech and turned and rolled just as if it had been alive. . . ."

In 1665 a terrible outbreak of plague decimated the population of England, claiming nearly 150,000 victims. One symptom of the disease was an acute drowsiness that brought an overwhelming desire for sleep. Since bodies were hurried out of the houses at night, it is hardly surprising that those deeply asleep might be taken for dead—especially as they were buried hastily in communal pits without the proper formalities of a funeral. . . .

Of Decomposition and Transients

Premature burial, therefore, is one logical explanation for bodies that have moved and twisted in their graves. Another is that a dead body shrinks naturally, and as the corpse shrinks, the hair and nails appear to grow longer. There are also medical explanations for such apparent phenomena as the scream that the body is supposed to utter as the stake is plunged through the heart. Finally, the soil in which a body is buried can explain why it remains so well preserved. For example, on the Greek island of Santorini, where vampires were said to be so abundant, the volcanic nature of the soil would help keep the bodies intact longer.

These explanations do not account for the reports of vampires who have left their graves and are seen outside them at night. Yet even here there is a straightforward answer suggested by Dennis Wheatley, a best-selling writer on the occult. In times of extreme poverty, beggars would take shelter in graveyards, and make family vaults or mausoleums their macabre homes. Driven by hunger, they would have to leave these tombs by night to forage for food in the neighborhood. If such figures were glimpsed in the moonlight it is understandable that they might be thought of as vampires. An empty grave can be explained simply as the work of a body snatcher who had stolen the corpse to sell for medical dissection.

Vampires of the Mind

All these logical explanations fail to account for the persistence of the vampire legend, however. It goes deeper. Indeed, much of the fascination for vampires lies in the subconscious.

On one level there is the basic desire for reunion with dead loved ones. "It is believed," wrote British psychologist Professor Ernest Jones in *On the Nightmare*, "that they [the dead] feel an overpowering impulse to return to the loved ones whom they had left. The deepest source of this projection is doubtless to be found in the wish that those who have departed should not forget us, a wish that ultimately springs from childhood memories of being left alone by the loved parent." He concludes, "The belief that the dead can visit their loved ones, especially by night, is met with over the whole world." It is certainly the case that the majority of reports show alleged vampires returning to their loved ones and families.

Psychic Vampires

What about the traditional symbolism of blood as the vital essence of life? To the vampire the sucking of blood is a form of transfusion, and this life restorer is a remedy that goes back through history. Early Australian tribes used to treat their sick by opening the veins of male friends, collecting the blood in a bowl, and feeding it to the invalid in its raw state.

Bloodsucking may also be an image for the way in which certain people seem to feed on the energy of others, draining them of vitality. Most of us have come across someone whom we might call a parasite, a sponger, or a leech. Vampire would be an equally suitable description. An encounter with such a person can leave us feeling absolutely exhausted. It has been noticed in hospitals that some people can even have this effect on machines, causing them to drop in electric current.

The draining of another's energy is particularly likely to happen in a marriage, family, or other close emotional relationship—traditionally the vampire's favorite feeding ground. There are also real cases of a strong personality exerting an unnatural influence over a weaker one. One example of this is how Ian Brady controlled Myra Hindley in their wholesale torture and killing of children in the British Moors Murders. Another is the power of Charles Manson over the group called his family. In this connection we might recall the vampire's reputed power to hypnotize a victim while draining its strengths.

Vampires as Symbols of Sexuality

Above all there is a powerful sexual element in vampirism, which is undoubtedly one of the main reasons for its continuing fascination. This aspect of the vampire theme was played down in the 19th century when, although cruelty and violence were acceptable topics for publication, sex was heavily censored. However, some Eastern European vampire tales state quite frankly that bloodsucking was not the only activity the vampire had in mind when he or she chose a victim. It is certainly part of the legend that male vampires prefer beautiful young girls, while female vampires practice their hypnotic charms on handsome young men.

The vampire's biting kiss on the victim's throat in order to suck out blood has an erotic and sadistic content that has not escaped the attention of psychologists. Ernest Jones says that "The act of sucking has a sexual significance from earliest infancy which is maintained throughout life in the form of kissing." A bite, according to Freud, is a part sadistic, part erotic kiss. Blood is also deeply linked with sexuality. "It has long been recognized by medico psychologists," wrote Montague Summers in his history of vampirism, "that there exists a definite connection between the fascination of blood and sexual excitement." Modern psychologists also note that blood and bloodletting are frequently associated with the erotic fantasies of their patients. . . .

We now see that there are psychological reasons for the appeal of the vampire as well as logical explanations for vampire beliefs. But the big question remains unanswered: are there really such things as vampires—not the living person who drains us of vitality, nor the occasional individual who develops a mania for blood, but the bloodsucking cousin of the ghost, the so-called living dead? As an expert on vampires, Montague Summers came to this conclusion: "Consciously or unconsciously it is realized that the vampire tradition contains far more truth than the ordinary individual cares to appreciate and acknowledge.". . .

Vampires and Missing Time

When someone dies, a close friend or relative frequently gets an instinctive feeling that the death has happened, even hundreds of miles away. Sometimes the death is dreamt of. Occasionally, the dying person is seen by another at the very moment of death. In a similar way the sighting of vampires could be a time lapse, a version of the experience known as *déjà vu* in which one feels one has been in a strange place before. Some people believe that the sighting of flying saucers is a look into the future when such transport will be common. Conversely, alleged glimpses of the Loch Ness Monster may be a look back into the prehistoric past when monster creatures abounded.

Such a case of time out of joint would help to explain the Irish legend of a funeral cortege which, having just buried their local priest in the neighboring hills, noticed a clerical figure coming toward them. As he passed, they were shocked to recognize the man they had just laid to rest. Hurrying to his home they found his mother in a state of extreme agitation because her dead son had appeared at the house an hour before. Had this happened in Eastern Europe, the priest might well have been dubbed a vampire, particularly if there were any other unusual or mysterious circumstances in the way he died.

Vampires as an Astral Projection

A more complex theory concerning the existence of vampires was put forward by the late Dion Fortune, a leading modern occultist. Like many occultists she believed in the *astral body*—the spiritual second body that can separate itself from the physical body and take on a life of its own. She maintained that by a trick of occultism, it is possible to prevent disintegration of the astral body after the death of the physical body. She referred to a case she had encountered involving some dead Hungarian soldiers who were reported to have become vampires, and to have made vampires of their victims. She suggested that these soldiers "maintained themselves in the etheric double [astral body] by vampirizing the wounded. Now vampirism is contagious; the person who is vampirized, being depleted of vitality, is a psychic vacuum, himself absorbing from anyone he comes across in order to refill his depleted sources of vitality. He soon learns by experience the tricks of a vampire without realizing their significance, and before he knows where he is, he is a full-blown vampire himself."

After death separation of the astral body from the physical body is permanent. But occultists believe that the astral body can also escape from the physical body during a person's life, and that it may take on some other form—that of a bird or animal, for example. Could this provide further grounds for a belief in the existence of vampires? Dion Fortune firmly believed in the ability of powerful feelings to create thought forms that possess a separate existence. Highly charged negative feelings might therefore cause the astral body to assume the form of an evil monster or ghost—possibly a vampire.

Discussing Dion Fortune's theory in *The Occult*, Colin Wilson agrees that "strange forces can erupt from the subconscious and take on apparently material shape." He quotes the story of a young Romanian peasant girl Eleonore Zugun. Eleonore showed a psychical investigator "devil's bites" on her hands and arms. As he sat with her she cried out, and marks of teeth appeared on the back of her hand, developing into bruises. A few minutes later she was bitten on the forearm, and the investigator could see deep teeth marks. Was this a ghost, asks Wilson, or Eleonore's own subconscious mind out of control? Perhaps it wasn't even Eleonore's mind, he suggests. "It might have been *somebody else's* mind."

"The subconscious mind is not simply a kind of deep seat repository of sunken memories and atavistic desires," says Wilson, "but of forces that can, under certain circumstances, manifest themselves in the physical world with a force that goes beyond anything the conscious mind could command." He feels that this might explain the mystery of vampires, and indeed of all so-called occult phenomena.

The Question Remains

Can a mental image be projected as a physical reality? Can the subconscious mind create monsters or ghosts that attack and destroy? Can the astral body of a dead person attach itself to a living person, feeding off him as a vampire in order to maintain life?

Many people would say that the only vampires we might possibly encounter are living people whose private fantasy life and peculiar aberration is that of the bloodsucking vampire. If this side of a person becomes dominant, he might even believe himself to be a vampire. If his fantasy assumes the shape of a wolf, he may act like a wolf. But the nagging question remains: is there ever a moment when that person actually *becomes* a vampire or a wolf, through some external influence we do not yet understand?

Vampires and the Facts of Decomposition

Paul Barber

Paul Barber is a research associate at the Fowler Museum of Cultural History at the University of California, Los Angeles, and is the author of *Vampires, Burial, and Death: Folklore and Reality*. In the following article, Barber argues that natural decomposition processes cause human corpses to exhibit some of the traditional symptoms of vampiric behavior related in eyewitness accounts and folklore. Decomposition can cause corpses to exhibit the pooling or leakage of blood, the sudden spasmodic movements of various muscles due to deterioration, and the unusual sounds of various gases escaping the body after death. Such phenomena would give a corpse the appearance of life. According to Barber, understanding decomposition processes provides an explanation for how people in ages past could have easily believed vampires to exist among their dead. Barber also discusses the ways in which belief systems involving vampires were strengthened through the dreams about dead loved ones returning from the grave as vampires. These dreams—which Barber believes explain the eyewitness accounts of vampires roaming villages in the night—combined with the visual evidence of natural decomposition to produce a volatile mix in the creation of a powerful myth. Barber concludes that the vampire is a figment of superstitious imaginings and incorrect conclusions. However, historically, the image of the vampire has necessarily provided a way for illiterate and uneducated people to explain events that have been, at any given time, unexplainable.

If a typical vampire of folklore were to come to your house this Halloween, you might open the door to encounter a plump Slavic fellow with long fingernails and a stubbly beard, his mouth and left eye open, his face ruddy and swollen. He would wear informal attire—a linen shroud—and he would look for all the world like a disheveled peasant. . . .

But in folklore, the undead are seemingly everywhere in the world, in a variety of disparate cultures. They are people who, having died before their time, are believed to return to life to bring death to their friends and neighbors.

We know the European version of the vampire best and have a number of eyewitness accounts telling of the "killing" of bodies believed to be vampires. When we read these reports carefully and compare their findings with what is now known about forensic pathology, we can see why people believed that corpses came to life and returned to wreak havoc on the local population. . . .

In the early 1730s, a group of Austrian medical officers were sent to the Serbian village of Medvegia to investigate some very strange accounts. A number of people in the village had died recently, and the villagers blamed the deaths on vampires. The first of these vampires, they said, had been a man named Arnold Paole, who had died some years before (by falling off a hay wagon) and had come back to haunt the living.

To the villagers, Paole's vampirism was clear: When they dug up his corpse, "they found that he was quite complete and undecayed, and that fresh blood had flowed from his eyes, nose, mouth, and ears; that the shirt, the covering, and the coffin were completely bloody; that the old nails on his hands and feet, along with the skin, had fallen off, and that new ones had grown; and since they saw from this that he was a true vampire, they drove a stake through his heart, according to their custom, whereby he gave an audible groan and bled copiously."

This new offensive by the vampires—the one that drew the medical officers to Medvegia—included an attack on a woman named Stanacka, who "lay down to sleep fifteen days ago, fresh and healthy, but at midnight she started up out of her sleep with a terrible cry, fearful and trembling and complained that she had been throttled by the son of a Haiduk by the name of Milloe, who had died nine weeks earlier, whereupon she had experienced a great pain in the chest and became worse hour by hour, until finally she died on the third day."

In their report, *Visum et Repertum (Seen and Discovered)*, the officers told not only what they had heard from the villagers but also, in admirable clinical detail, what they themselves had seen when they exhumed and dissected the bodies of the supposed victims of the vampire. Of one corpse, the authors observed, "After the opening of the body there was found in the *cavitate pectoris* [chest cavity] a quantity of fresh extravascular blood. The *vasa* [vessels] of the *arteriae* and *venae,* like the *ventriculis cordis,* were not, as is usual, filled with coagulated blood, and the whole *viscera,* that is, the *pulmo* [lung], *hepar* [liver], *stomachus, lien* [spleen], *et intestina* were quite fresh as they would be in a healthy person." But while baffled by the events, the medical officers did not venture opinions as to their meaning.

Modern Medicine Provides Some Explanations

Modern scholars generally disregard such accounts—and we have many of them—because they invariably contain "facts" that are not believable, such as the claim that the dead Arnold Paole, exhumed forty days after his burial, groaned when a stake was driven into him. If that is untrue—and it surely seems self-evident that it must be untrue—then the rest of the account seems suspect.

Yet these stories invariably contain details that could only be known by someone who had exhumed a decomposing body. The flaking away of the skin described in the account of Arnold Paole is a phenomenon that forensic pathologists refer to as "skin slippage." Also, pathologists say that it is no surprise that Paole's "nails had fallen away," for that too is a normal event. (The Egyptians knew this and dealt with it either by tying the nails onto the mummified corpse or by attaching them with little golden thimbles.) The reference to "new nails" is presumably the interpretation of the glossy nail bed underneath the old nails.

Such observations are inconvenient if the vampire lore is considered as something made up out of whole cloth. But since the exhumations actually took place, then the question must be, how did our sources come to the conclusions they came to? That issue is obscured by two centuries of fictional vampires, who are much better known than the folkloric variety. A few distinctions are in order. . . .

Signs of Vampirism in Corpses and Nature

The color red is related to the undead. Decomposing corpses often acquire a ruddy color, and this was generally taken for evidence of vampirism. Thus, the folkloric vampire is never pale, as one would expect of a corpse; his face is commonly described as florid or of a healthy color or dark, and this may be attributed to his habit of drinking blood. . . .

In various parts of Europe, vampires, or revenants, were held responsible for any number of untoward events. They tipped over Gypsy caravans in Serbia, made loud noises on the frozen sod roofs of houses in Iceland (supposedly by beating their heels against them), caused epidemics, cast spells on crops, brought on rain and hail, and made cows go dry. All these activities attributed to vampires do occur; storms and scourges come and go, crops don't always thrive, cows do go dry. Indeed, the vampire's crimes are persistently "real-life" events. The issue often is not whether an event occurred but why it was attributed to the machinations of the vampire, an often invisible villain.

Bodies continue to be active long after death, but we moderns distinguish between two types of activity: that which we bring about by our will (in life) and that which is caused by other entities, such as microorganisms (in death). Because we regard only the former as "our" activity, the body's posthumous movements, changes in dimension, or the like are not real for us, since we do not will them. For the most part, however, our ancestors made no such distinction. To them, if after death the body changed in color, moved, bled, and so on (as it does), then it continued to experience a kind of life. Our view of death has made it difficult for us to understand earlier views, which are often quite pragmatic.

Much of what a corpse "does" results from misunderstood processes of decomposition. Only in detective novels does this process proceed at a predictable rate. So when a body that had seemingly failed to decompose came to the attention of the populace, theories explaining the apparent anomaly were likely to spring into being. . . .

But however mythical the vampire was, the corpses that were taken for vampires were very real. And many of the mysteries of vampire lore clear up when we examine the legal and medical evidence surrounding these exhumations. "Not without astonishment," says an observer at the exhumation of a Serbian vampire in 1725, "I saw some fresh blood in his mouth, which, according to the common observation, he had sucked from the people killed by him." Similarly, in *Visum et Repertum*, we are told that the people exhuming one body were surprised by a "plumpness" they asserted had come to the corpse in the grave. Our sources deduced a cause-and-effect relationship from these two observations. The vampire was larger than he was because he was full to bursting with the fresh blood of his victims.

The observations are clinically accurate: as a corpse decomposes, it normally bloats (from the gases given off by decomposition), while the pressure from the bloating causes blood from the lungs to emerge at the mouth. The blood is real, it just didn't come from "victims" of the deceased.

But how was it that Arnold Paole, exhumed forty days after his death, groaned when his exhumers drove a stake into him? The peasants of Medvegia assumed that if the corpse groaned, it must still be alive. But a corpse does emit sounds, even when it is only moved, let alone if a stake were driven into it. This is because the compression of the chest cavity forces air past the glottis, causing a sound similar in quality and origin to the groan or cry of a living person. Pathologists shown such accounts point out that a corpse that did not emit such sounds when a stake was driven into it would be unusual.

Expect the Unexpected

To vampire killers who are digging up a corpse, anything unexpected is taken for evidence of vampirism. [Augustine] Calmet, an eighteenth-century French ecclesiastic, described people digging up corpses "to see if they can find any of the usual marks which leads them to conjecture that they are the parties who molest the living, as the mobility and suppleness of the limbs, the fluidity of the blood, and the flesh remaining uncorrupted." A vampire, in other words, is a corpse that lacks rigor mortis, has fluid blood, and has not decomposed. As it happens, these distinctions do not narrow the field very much: Rigor mortis is a temporary condition, liquid blood is not at all unusual in a corpse (hence the "copious bleeding" mentioned in the account of Arnold Paole), and burial slows down decomposition drastically (by a factor of eight, according to a standard textbook on forensic pathology). This being the case, exhumations often yielded a corpse that nicely fit the local model of what a vampire was.

Nightmares in Disguise

None of this explains yet another phenomenon of the vampire lore—the attack itself. To get to his victim, the vampire is often said to emerge at night from a tiny hole in the grave, in a form that is invisible to meet people (sorcerers have made a good living tracking down and killing such vampires). The modern reader may reject out of hand the hypothesis that a dead man, visible or not, crawled out of his grave and attacked the young woman Stanacka as related in *Visum et Repertum*. Yet in other respects, these accounts have been quite accurate.

Note the sequence of events: Stanacka is asleep, the attack takes place, and she wakes up. Since Stanacka was asleep during the attack, we can only conclude that we are looking at a culturally conditioned interpretation of a nightmare—a real event with a fanciful interpretation.

The vampire does have two forms: one of them the body in the grave; the other—and this is the mobile one—the image, or "double," which here appears as a dream. While we interpret this as an event that takes place within the mind of the dreamer, in nonliterate cultures the dream is more commonly viewed as either an invasion by the spirits of whatever is dreamed about (and these can include the dead) or evidence that the dreamer's soul is taking a nocturnal journey.

Evidence Appears to Support Eyewitness Account

In many cultures, the soul is only rather casually attached to its body, as is demonstrated by its habit of leaving the body entirely during sleep or unconsciousness or death. The changes that occur during such conditions—the lack of responsiveness, the cessation or slowing of breathing and pulse—are attributed to the soul's departure. When the soul is identified with the image of the body, it may make periodic forays into the minds of others when they dream. The image is the essence of the person, and its presence in the mind of another is evidence that body and soul are separated. Thus, one reason that the dead are believed to live on is that their image can appear in people's dreams and memories even after death. . . .

When Stanacka claimed she was attacked by Milloe, she was neither lying nor even making an especially startling accusation. Her subsequent death (probably from some form of epidemic disease; others in the village were dying too) was sufficient proof to her friends and relatives that she had in fact been attacked by a dead man, just as she had said.

This is why our sources tell us seemingly contradictory

facts about the vampire. His body does not have to leave the grave to attack the living, yet the evidence of the attack—the blood he has sucked from his victims—is to be seen on the body. At one and the same time he can be both in the grave in his physical form and out of it in his spirit form. . . .

Fear Responsible for Belief in Vampires

Perhaps foremost among the reasons for the urgency with which vampires were sought—and found—was sheer terror. To understand its intensity we need only recall the realities that faced our informants. Around them people were dying in clusters, by agencies that they did not understand. As they were well aware, death could be extremely contagious: if a neighbor died, they might be next. They were afraid of nothing less than death itself. For among many cultures it was death that was thought to be passed around, not viruses and bacteria. Contagion was meaningful and deliberate, and its patterns were based on values and vendettas, not on genetic predisposition or the domestic accommodations of the plague-spreading rat fleas. Death came from the dead who, through jealousy, anger, or longing, sought to bring the living into their realm. And to prevent this, the living attempted to neutralize or propitiate the dead until the dead became powerless—not only when they stopped entering dreams but also when their bodies stopped changing and were reduced to inert bones. This whole phenomenon is hard for us to understand because although death is as inescapable today as it was then, we no longer personify its causes.

In recent history, the closest parallel to this situation may be seen in the AIDS epidemic, which has caused a great deal of fear, even panic, among people who, for the time being at least, know little about the nature of the disease. In California, for instance, there was an attempt to pass a law re-

quiring the quarantine of AIDS victims. Doubtless the fear
will die down if we gain control over the disease—but what
would it be like to live in a civilization in which all diseases
were just as mysterious? Presumably one would learn—as
was done in Europe in past centuries—to shun the dead as
potential bearers of death.

Psychological Explanations for Vampirism

J. Gordon Melton

J. Gordon Melton is director of the Institute for the Study of American Religion in Evanston, Illinois. He has written widely on the subject of religions and religious freedom, issues of morality, and on the subject of the occult. The following essay is taken from Melton's *The Vampire Book*, a thoroughly researched encyclopedia on the vampire in history, literature, film, music, science, and culture. In this essay, Melton provides a readable overview of psychological theories involving the vampire myth. Beginning with Sigmund Freud in the twentieth century, psychologists turned their efforts to the study of the unconscious mind and the ways in which humans deal with emotional and sexual desires. Many of these desires are repressed, buried in the mind, out of a fear that the individual who tries to fulfill them will be perceived negatively in society. The image of the vampire occurs in dreams as a symbol for many of these

J. Gordon Melton, *The Vampire Book: The Encyclopedia of the Undead*. Detroit: Visible Ink Press, 1994. Copyright © 1994 by Visible Ink Press. Reproduced by permission.

desires, particularly those involving power, immortality, loneliness, and sexuality. Melton carefully presents each psychological theory, including appropriate examples. Whether the reader agrees with the theories or not, they provide intriguing evidence that the vampire has never existed in the supernatural realm, but only as a man-made creation whose function is merely to symbolize the darkness in all of us.

Through the twentieth century the psychological element of the vampire myth repeatedly captured the attention, even fascination, of psychological researchers. The widespread presence of the vampire image in human cultures led some psychologists to call the vampire an archetype—an intrapsychic psychological structure grounded in the collective unconscious. The differing major psychoanalytic interpretations help us understand the compelling fascination with narratives and images grounded in vampire mythology. This mythology rests on central metaphors of the mysterious power of human blood, images of the undead, forbidden and sexualized longings, and the ancient idea that evil is often hard to detect in the light of day. Humans have long felt that there is a sense in which evil operates like a contagious disease, spreading through defilement caused by direct contact with a carrier of a supernatural "toxin."

The Theories of Sigmund Freud

Prior to Freud's development of psychoanalysis, even sophisticated psychologies tended to associate the realm of the undead with premodern demonological mythologies. Freudian thought legitimized the human fantasies of the undead as a topic for serious scientific research. Freud developed a modern map of the unconscious, which he saw as a repository of denied desires, impulses, and wishes of a sexual and sometimes destructively aggressive nature. In sleep we view the unconscious as a landscape inhabited by those aspects of life that go on living, the realm of the un-dead spoken through dreams. [This idea is explored in more detail in the essay by Ernest Jones, also in this chapter.] Ac-cording to Freudian psychoanalysis, vampire narratives ex-press in complex form the fascination—both natural and unnatural—which the living take in death and the dead. From Freud's point of view, "All human experiences of mor-bid dread [the extreme terror of something gruesome or un-wholesome] signify the presense of repressed [buried] sex-ual and agressive wishes, and in vampirism we see these repressed wishes becoming plainly visible." Freudians em-phasize the ways in which ambivalence permeates vampire stories. Death wishes coexist with the longing for immor-tality. Greed and sadistic agression coexist with a compul-sively possessive expression of desire. Images of deep and shared guilt coexist with those of virginal innocence and vulnerability.

The Oedipal Vampire

Freud and his followers noted the ways in which vampire stories reflect the unconscious world of polymorphous per-verse infantile sexuality. . . . According to Freud, the Oedipus complex emerges between the ages of three and five and is responsible for much unconscious guilt. Oedipal rivalry with fathers causes castration anxiety in males. Both males and fe-males experience feelings of aggression toward the parent of the same sex and feelings of possessive erotic desire toward the parent of the opposite sex. Since conscious awareness of these feelings and associated wishes raises the anxiety level of the child to unacceptable levels, ego defenses come into play to prevent the conscious mind from becoming more aware of these dangerous impulses. From the Freudian point of view, it is the function of dreams to disguise these wishes into more acceptable forms that will not wake the dreamer from sleep. Thus, a competent dream interpretation can trace dream images back to the unacceptable Oedipal wishes that underlie them. Following this belief, the vampire image is a fantasy image related to these wishes.

A classical Freudian interpretation of the vampire legend, therefore, seeks to discern the same denied Oedipal wishes in the story. Here the blending of sexuality and aggression in the vampire attack is seen as suggestive of the child's interpretation of the primal scene (the parents having sexual intercourse). That is, the male child often fantasizes sexual contact between his parents as causing harm to the mother. . . .

Clearly, Freud and his early followers were right in their assumption that the vampire myth was grounded in archaic images of repressed longings and fears. However, the classical Freudian interpretation—while containing some helpful insights—was a gross oversimplification of the psychological contents of vampire narratives. Carl Jung offered the first powerful alternative to early Freudian views.

The Theories of Carl Jung

Jungian psychoanalysts point to the worldwide interest in the vampire as evidence of its archetypal nature. From a Jungian perspective, the myriad varieties of vampire narratives found cross-culturally throughout history indicate that these images are not merely by-products of personal experience but are grounded in species-wide psychological structures. In other words, vampire images reflect significant experiences and issues that are universal in human lives around the world. In short, there is something about the vampire that we already understand intuitively—with the knowledge coming from deep within our psyche.

Jung believed that the vampire image could be understood as an expression of what he termed the "shadow," those aspects of the self that the conscious ego was unable to recognize. Some aspects of the shadow were positive. But usually the shadow contained repressed wishes, anti-social impulses, morally questionable motives, childish fantasies of a grandiose nature, and other traits felt to be shameful. As Jung put it:

> The shadow is a moral problem that challenges the whole ego-personality, for no one can become conscious of the shadow without considerable moral effort. To become conscious of it involves recognizing the dark aspects of the personality as present and real.

The vampire could be seen as a projection of that aspect of the personality, which according to the conscious mind should be dead but nevertheless lives. In this way Jung interpreted the vampire as an unconscious complex that could gain control over the psyche, taking over the conscious mind like an enchantment or spell. And even when we were not overwhelmed by this unconscious complex, its presence led us to project the content of the complex onto characters in a vampire narrative. Of social importance, the image of the vampire in popular culture serves us as a useful scapegoat since—through the mechanism of projection—the vampire allows us to disown the negative aspects of our personalities. . . .

This Jungian interpretation of the vampire image provided significant insight into the enormous popularity of vampire stories. From this point of view, a vampire lives within each of us. We project this inner reality on both male and female persons, members of other "tribes" and ethnic groups. We all have a dim awareness that this demonic yet tragic figure is real. However, we usually fail to grasp that this outer image is an expression of an inner reality—a reality that is elusive, threatening to self and others, and that can be effectively engaged only through a combination of empathy and heroic effort.

The Psychic Vampire and Narcissistic Personality Disorder

Jung did not limit his discussion to what would be an over-simplification by suggesting that vampiric traits in others result entirely from our projections. He observed that auto-erotic, autistic, or otherwise narcissistic personality traits can result in a personality that is in fact predatory, anti-social, and parasitic on the life energy of others. In contemporary psychology and psychiatry this type of personality is called a "narcissistic personality disorder." This clinical syndrome contains the most important clues to the psychological reality represented in the vampire image.

Otto Kernberg noted that narcissistic personalities are characterized by a "very inflated concept of themselves and an inordinate need for tribute from others." Capable of only a shallow emotional life they have difficulty experiencing any empathy for the feelings of others. Their ability to enjoy life, except for their experiences of their own grandiose fantasies and the tributes that they can manipulate others into giving them, is severely limited. They easily become restless and bored unless new sources are feeding their self-esteem. They envy what others possess and tend to idealize the few people from whom they desire food for their narcissistic needs. They depreciate and treat with contempt any from whom they do not expect nurturance. According to Kernberg, "their relationships with other people are clearly exploitative and parasitic." Kernberg's description of the narcissistic personality sounds as if it were crafted to describe vampires:

It is as if they feel they have the right to control and possess others and to exploit them without guilt feelings—and behind the surface, which very often is charming and engaging, one senses coldness and ruthlessness.

Jungian interpreters often highlight the parallels between the vampire image and the characteristics of narcissistic psychopathology. Daryl Coats, for example, has noted that the vampire is both narcissistic [having an excess of admiration for oneself] and autistic [possession of an abnormal subjectivity]. He emphasizes that the vampire experiences "narcissistic self-destruction as a result of their intensely selfish desires." Jungian analyst Julia McAfee has focused on the vampire as an image of the shadow of the narcissistic mother. The narcissistic mother, while appearing on the surface to have good will and a nurturing attitude toward the child, in fact drains the energy of the child and weakens the child through subtle (and not so subtle) emotional exploitation. This pattern provides insight into the psychological experiences that underlie the numerous folktales of vampires preying on children. Vampiric parents have always been a widespread human phenomenon—and there is reason to believe that the incidence of such predatory behavior toward children is increasing. . . .

Causes and Symptoms of Narcissistic Personality Disorder

What goes wrong to cause an individual to develop a narcissistic personality disorder? As [Heinz] Kohut emphasized, the development of a "normal" personality requires a creative interplay between the innate potentials of the child's self and the emotional environment that is created by those who are the primary caregivers of the child. . . .

Kohut asserted that an inadequate nurturing environment causes significant damage in the form of "narcissistic wounds." The development of the self is arrested and the emerging self is left in a weakened condition in an ongoing struggle with overwhelming longings and unmet emotional needs. When normal development is disturbed in this way, the resulting state of emotional disequilibrium necessitates that the individual seek to compensate for the resulting deficit or weakness in the structure of the self. Therefore, the person who has not successfully built a psychological internal structure remains pathologically needy and dependent upon others to perform functions he or she can not execute. Others must be "used" in various ways to bolster a fragile sense of self and to attempt to fill an inner emptiness. This primal dependency is at the root of "vampiric" predatory patterns in relationships.

Symptoms resulting from such emotional disturbances have characteristic features. Patients often report feeling depressed, depleted, and drained of energy. They report feelings of emptiness, dulled emotions, inhibited initiative, and not being completely real. At work they may find themselves constricted in creativity and unproductive. In social interaction they may have difficulty in forming and sustaining interpersonal relationships. They may become involved in delinquent and anti-social activities. They often lack empathy for the feelings and needs of others, have attacks of uncontrolled rage or pathological lying. Often a person with such narcissistic wounds will become hypochondriacally preoccupied with bodily states. They will experience bodily sensations of being cold, drained and empty. These clinical descriptions, of course, parallel some of the major symptoms of the victims of vampires as described in vampire narratives. . . .

In surveying the development of the major psychoanalytic perspectives on the vampire, the attempt was made to trace the manner in which each school of thought, out of its understanding of fundamental psychodynamic processes, sought to interpret vampirism. Each of these perspectives contributed to the understanding of the rich mythological and symbolic narratives of vampire lore and one by one built the foundation upon which the more promising contemporary interpretation by self-psychology, which views the vampire as a primary icon representing essential aspects of narcissistic psychopathology, rests. Self-psychology calls attention to the significance of inner emptiness, the longing for emotional nutriments that can prevent disintegration of the self, and the resulting envy that sees such nutriments (the Good) in others and wishes to take it from them. Contemporary psychoanalytic self-psychology in the tradition of Heinz Kohut and Ernest Wolf, in offering a more complete psychological understanding of the origins, major forms, and manifestations of such vampiric psychological illness, also provides the necessary therapeutic insights and techniques needed if healing for vampiric and vampirized personalities is to occur.

The Vampire: A Nightmare from the Unconscious Mind

Ernest Jones

A psychoanalyst who worked closely with Sigmund Freud, Ernest Jones is most well known for his book *On the Nightmare*, from which the following excerpt is taken. In it, Jones argues that humans create monsters as a way to help explain, or assign responsibility for, repressed desires and fears created by extreme emotions of love and hate. Acting on these desires or fears would mean admitting that a dark, or less socially acceptable, side of human nature exists. In an attempt to avoid this confrontation, responsibility for this darkness is projected onto the monsters created in the imagination. Jones' point is that repressing the fears or desires does not make them go away. They are simply buried in the unconscious mind, where they surface in the form of the nightmare. Jones defines the basic characteristics of the nightmare and demonstrates how the image of the vampire works within nightmares as a powerful symbol for many unfulfilled desires and fears related to sexuality. In contrast to the traditional belief in the supernatural existence of the vampire, Jones' theories suggest that the vampire does not exist as a physical or ghostly being, but is instead a creation of the human mind.

It is generally recognized that the Nightmare has exercised a greater influence on waking phantasy than any other dream. This is especially true of the origin of the belief in evil spirits and monsters. [In his book, *Myths and Dreams*, Edward] Clodd, for instance, speaks of 'the intensified form of dreaming called "nightmare", when hideous spectres sit upon the breast, stopping breath and paralysing motion, and to which is largely due the creation of the vast army of nocturnal demons that fill the folk-lore of the world.' . . .

All this is not surprising when we remember that the vividness of Nightmares far transcends that of ordinary dreams. Waller says: 'The degree of consciousness during a paroxysm [sudden fit] of Nightmare is so much greater than ever happens in a dream, that the person who has had a vision of this kind cannot easily bring himself to acknowledge the deceit.' . . .

Characteristics of the Nightmare and the Power of Repressed Desires

Before we discuss the part that the Nightmare has played in giving rise to superstitious ideas we must first say something about the Nightmare itself. The three cardinal features of a typical Nightmare are: (1) agonizing dread; (2) a suffocating sense of oppression at the chest; and (3) a conviction of helpless paralysis. Less conspicuous features are an outbreak of cold sweat, convulsive palpitation of the heart, and sometimes a flow of seminal or vaginal secretion, or even a paralysis of the sphincters. . . .

[The] Nightmare is a form of anxiety attack, that is essentially due to an intense mental conflict centreing around some repressed component of the psycho-sexual instinct, characteristically a re-activation of the normal incest wishes of infancy, and that it may be evoked by any peripheral stimuli that serve to arouse associatively this body of repressed feeling . . .

When the repression is slight, . . . an erotic desire, perhaps one which would be suppressed in waking moments, can come to imaginary fulfilment in a dream. When the repression is greater the dream contains a mixture of pleasurable sensation and of discomfort or fear. When the repression is greater still the fear may overshadow the voluptuous feeling, and in the extreme case of the typical Nightmare it entirely replaces it. This circumstance, that an admixture of erotic and apprehensive emotions may be found in all degrees, we shall see to be extensively paralleled by the various myths and . . . superstitious beliefs connected with the Nightmare theme. . . .

Monsters Symbolize Fears in Dreams

The reason why the object seen in a Nightmare is frightful or hideous is simply that the representation of the underlying wish is not permitted in its naked form, so that the dream is a compromise of the wish on the one hand, and on the other of the intense fear belonging to the inhibition. . . .

The different conceptions of impossible monsters are very suggestive of a source in the experiences of anxiety dreams. This group of ideas is very extensive. The belief in the real existence of such monsters has held its own well into modern times and cannot yet be said to have died out, even amongst civilized nations. . . .

Webster's *International Dictionary* defines a Vampire as: 'A blood-sucking ghost or re-animated body of a dead person; a soul or re-animated body of a dead person believed to come from the grave and wander about by night sucking the blood of persons asleep, causing their death.' The *Century Dictionary* describes a Vampire as: 'A kind of spectral body which, according to a superstition existing among the Slavic and other races on the Lower Danube, leaves the grave during the night and maintains a semblance of life by sucking the warm blood of men and women while they are asleep. Dead wizards, werewolves, heretics and other outcasts become vampires, as do also the illegitimate offspring of parents themselves illegitimate, and anyone killed by a vampire.'

The two essential characteristics of a true Vampire are thus his origin in a dead person and his habit of sucking blood from a living one, usually with fatal effect. It will be expedient to treat them first separately.

Relationship Between the Living and the Dead

Interest of the living in the dead, whether in the body or in the spirit, is an inexhaustible theme, only a small part of which can be considered here. A continued relation between the living and dead may be regarded in two ways, and each of these from the obverse and reverse. On the one hand it may be desired, and this may result either in the living being drawn to the dead or in the dead being drawn back to the living; on the other hand it may be feared, which may also have the same two effects. In the Ghoul idea a living person visits the body of the dead; the Vampire idea is more elaborate, for here the dead first visits the living and then draws him into death, being re-animated himself in the process.

We shall see that several different emotions—love, guilt

and hate—impel towards a belief in the idea of reunion with the dead and in the idea with which we are particularly concerned, that of the return of the dead from the grave. The simplest case of all is where someone longs for the return of a dear lost one, but the greater part of our present problem is taken up with various motives that are supposed to actuate a dead person to return to the living. This latter group is so firmly bound up with the point of view of the corpse that it sometimes needs an effort to remember that they can only represent ideas projected on to him from the minds of the living. In this process, as so commonly with projection, the mechanism of identification is mostly at work; it is as though the living person whose unconscious wishes have been exemplified by the life and conduct of the recently deceased felt that if *he* were dead he would not be able to rest in his grave and would be impelled by various motives to return.

We shall divide into two broad groups the motives urging to re-union, and particularly to return from the grave: they may be called love and hate respectively.

Vampires and Love

That *Love* should concern itself with the re-union of parted lovers, even when the parting has been brought about by death, is natural enough. The derivatives of this theme, however, prove on examination to be unexpectedly complex. To begin with, the wish for the reunion may be expressed directly on the part of the living or it may be ascribed by projection to the dead. We shall consider first the former of these. The simplest expression of this is the aching longing to meet once more the lost one, a wish commonly gratified in dreams, which reaches its greatest intensity between lovers, married partners or children and parents. . . .

As has been said, the wish for re-union is often ascribed to the dead by the mechanism of projection. It is then believed that they feel an overpowering impulse to return to the loved ones whom they had left. The deepest source of this projection is doubtless to be found in the wish that those who have departed should not forget us, a wish that ultimately springs from childhood memories of being left alone by the loved parent. The belief that the dead can visit their loved ones, especially by night is met with over the whole world. . . .

We evidently have here a reason why Vampires always visit relatives first, particularly their married partners, a feature on which most descriptions dwell. . . .

Possession Through Death

We have next to mention a still more remarkable perversion of the love-instinct, namely, the wish to die together with the person one loves. . . . The sources of this wish are, as might perhaps be expected, very complicated, and I propose to say only a little about them here. The clearest of them is the sure feeling of definiteness and permanence that death offers: what one has in death one has for ever. . . .

Psycho-analysis has shown that this feature of insatiability and of insistence on exclusive possession is particularly urgent with those who have not succeeded in emancipating themselves from the infantile desire to make a test case of their first love problem, that of incest with the mother and rivalry with the father. Death, which so often in infancy means little more than departure, can then come to signify simply setting forth with the loved mother away from the disturbing influence of the hated father.

This love *motif* can, however, especially when in a state of repression, regress to an earlier form of sexuality, particularly to the sadistic-masochistic phase of development. It was remarked above that the masochistic side of a personality tends to regard the idea of Death as an aggressive onslaught, and the same is even truer of the idea of a dead person. A dead person who loves will love for ever and will never be weary of giving and receiving caresses. . . .

On the other hand the dead being allows everything, can offer no resistance, and the relationship has none of the inconvenient consequences that sexuality may bring in its train in life. The phantasy of loving such a being can therefore make a strong appeal to the sadistic side of the sexual instinct. . . .

The Vampire and Hate

We divided the motives impelling to re-union with the dead into two, those concerned with *Love* and with *Hate* respectively, and we have now to turn our attention to the second of these two groups. Though it is at least as important as the other motive, there is less to be said about it for the simple reason that it is far less complex. The mechanism is the same as that of the terrors of childhood, *i.e.* the fear of retaliation for wrong-doing or for wicked thoughts. Someone who has a repressed hatred—not an ordinary, conscious one—is apt to have bad dreams, or even a dread of ghosts, indicating his fear of being appropriately punished by the person to whom he had wished ill. These evil wishes play an enormously important part in the unconscious mind and ultimately emanate from the hostile 'death-wishes' nourished by the child against the disturbing parent or other rival. The guilty conscience resulting from such wishes against those who are otherwise objects of affection naturally brings the thought that if they really died, and the evil wishes were thus fulfilled, they would surely return from the grave to haunt and torture their 'murderer'. It is largely because such wishes are so common in the unconscious that the prevailing attitude towards the supernatural is one of fear or even terror. We have here another reason, in addition to the one formerly adduced, why a Vampire is so prone to visit his nearest relatives . . .

As is intelligible from daily experience, traces are plainly to be found in this set of beliefs of endeavours to shift the sense of guilt arising from repressed hostility. The most typical method is to displace it by projection on to the dead person himself, who is supposed to be unable to rest in peace because of his uneasy conscience. A person who is cursed . . . is believed to become a Vampire after death, the assumption being that he would not have been cursed had he not been a wicked person, so that the person cursing was fully justified in doing so. That is probably why the most effective curses and bans are those of a person of respect such as a father or godfather, above all those of a priest. In spite of these endeavours, however, the psychological fact remains and must be faced, that the person who dreads the Vampire is the person really afflicted by guilt. . . .

This theme of guiltiness leads us to the perception that the two fundamental motives of love and hate, *i.e.* the sexual and hostile impulses, meet at this nodal point. To put the matter simply, love leads to hate and hate leads to guilt. This reproduces the primordial triangular situation through which every individual has to pass in infancy, typically loving the parent of the opposite sex and hating that of the same sex. In the present context both of these emotional attitudes are projected on to the Vampire, whose sense of guilt is then supposed to impel him to allay it by glutting them in the way we have seen described. . . .

Beyond a Psychological Perspective: Some Other Ideas

Oddly enough, this is the only psychological explanation of the Vampire superstition that has ever been put forward; other explanations have mostly regarded the belief as a true one and have merely tried to show why it is true. This paucity of psychological explanation in itself shows that essential factors must have been overlooked hitherto, and it is hoped that the present study will contribute something to our understanding of them. There are two other facts of reality that have also been adduced to explain, or rather to justify, the Vampire belief: they are the occurrence of epidemic mortality, especially in association with the idea of foul smell, and the fact that in various circumstances decomposition after death can be very much delayed. Now a general popular tendency may readily be remarked to rationalize all superstitions by explaining them in terms of reality, though the slightest investigation shows that such explanations always leave the essentials unexplained. For instance, to say that the notion of its being unlucky to walk under a ladder simply proceeds from the observation that something may be dropped on to one so doing neither accounts for the distribution of the fear—for it cannot be supposed that only those who have the fear are the only people who have made this observation; on the contrary, it is more often quoted by those who are free from the fear—nor for the demonstrable association between this fear and that of passing through holes in general. And in the present case the three facts just mentioned—burial alive, epidemic mortality and delayed decomposition—in no way in themselves explain why a dead body should change into an animal, fly through the air and commit sexual excesses with sleeping people. Other factors must obviously be at work, and these we maintain are the essential ones. Psycho-analysis, both of superstitious beliefs—general or individual—and of other similar mental processes, shows that the essential factors are much more dynamic than mere observation of external phenomena. The unconscious tendencies at work in the construction of these beliefs simply fortify and justify them by any rationalistic means they can seize on. It is the capacity for immediate and intuitive insight into this way in which the mind functions that distinguishes a psychological mentality from others.

The motives of love and hate discussed in this article show what extremely complex and what fundamental emotions are at work in the construction and maintenance of the Vampire superstition. It is one more product of the deepest conflicts that determine human development and fate—those concerned with the earliest relationships to the parents.

Rare Disorders Explain Vampirism

Jill Burcum

Readable and well informed, the following article by Jill Burcum provides a brief overview of recent medical research that seeks to explain the vampire phenomenon documented in the eyewitness accounts. According to Burcum, medical experts have long been interested in trying to find some medical or physiological explanation for vampire accounts throughout history. Research over the last twenty years suggests that both "furious rabies" and porphyria, a rare genetic blood disease, cause symptoms and behaviors similar to those displayed by the vampires described in eyewitness accounts and traditional folk stories. Researchers argue that the discovery of these diseases and their resulting symptoms and behaviors perhaps caused communities to assign the label of vampire mistakenly to unfortunate individuals suffering from these disorders.

To most of the world, vampires are the stuff of movies and the cause of an unsettling shiver when passing by a cemetery late at night. But to scientists, Dracula and his bloodthirsty brethren are an old myth just begging for a 20th century explanation.

In an age of electron microscopes and MRIs [magnetic resolution imagery], the vampire remains the focus of a surprising amount of scientific speculation. Type the word "vampire" into Medline or any other medical database and several dozen references turn up. Although some are in fringe publications, a fair number are found in prestigious journals. Vampires even have been the subject of talks at major scientific meetings.

"I'm not sure why this intrigues scientists, but it seems to from time to time," says Paul Barber, a researcher at a University of California–Los Angeles museum and author of a book on the origins of the vampire myth. "Perhaps they're interested in applying what we know today to explain a myth that's scared people for centuries."

How do scientists explain the vampire legend? Answers vary, but many theories focus on physical disease. The idea is that certain disorders could have given people with the illnesses a vampire-like appearance. In the isolated villages of ancient and medieval Europe, where the vampire myth was born, the appearances of these victims could have led frightened and uneducated peasants to believe these monsters existed.

Although several diseases have been offered as explanations, two come up most often: rabies and a group of blood disorders called porphyrias. Of these two, rabies is the focus of the most recent scientific explanation.

In the September 1998 journal *Neurology*, Spanish physician Juan Gomez-Alonso proposed that vampires were really victims of a type of rabies called furious rabies.

Furious rabies usually is transferred to humans by an animal bite, Gomez-Alonso writes. That matches folklore of how vampires attacked. In certain cases, symptoms of furious rabies closely match traits typically ascribed to vampires, including clenched teeth, retracted lips, hypersexuality, frothing at the mouth and vomiting of bloody fluids. Victims of furious rabies also are known to be highly excitable, especially around mirrors, and to rush at those who approach and try to bite them.

"Much evidence supports that rabies could have played a key role in the generation of the vampire legend," Gomez-Alonso writes.

Other proponents of the rabies theory have made public their ideas in medical journals. In a letter published in the *Annals of Internal Medicine* in 1992, a Denmark physician concluded that the vampire of legend "could very well have been a poor, rabid peasant with a stake driven through his heart."

Although not a vampire enthusiast, rabies expert Dr. Tim Schacker of the University of Minnesota says rabies is an interesting take on vampires.

"It's a reasonable hypothesis," he said. "It'll never be proven, but why not consider it? Many viral infections have been around since antiquity."

Porphyria: The Vampire Disease

Porphyrias, a rare group of blood disorders sometimes offered as a vampire explanation, have generally fallen out of favor as a vampire theory, according to *The Vampire Book: Encyclopedia of the Undead* [by J. Gordon Melton]. However, it's probably the only one ever discussed at a major scientific meeting.

In 1985, at a national conference of the American Association for the Advancement of Science, Canadian researcher David Dolphin received national publicity when he proposed that vampires of folklore were really people with porphyrias.

Porphyrias result from the body's inability to make heme—the part of the blood that carries oxygen. Without heme, chemicals build up under the skin, causing it to become extremely sensitive to sunlight. In addition to painful skin lesions, porphyrias can cause excessive hair growth on the face, arms, hands and legs. The teeth and eyes also may develop a reddish hue. All of these symptoms, especially the heightened sun sensitivity, are vampire characteristics in folklore.

Dolphin hypothesized that the changes caused by the disease could have frightened peasants into believing that they had seen a vampire. His talk, which received widespread publicity, generated controversy when people with the disorder protested that others now thought of them as monsters.

"As theories go, no one is promoting that any more," said Barber, who is considered a vampire expert after publication of his book *Vampires, Burial and Death: Folklore and Reality.*

Barber has a different take on the vampire myth. An expert on German folklore, he said most scientists offering vampire theories are using such fictional monsters as Braim Stoker's Dracula, as their guide to vampire behavior and appearance. That makes their theories flawed, he said.

The vampires of European folklore traveled the countryside as spirits—not as actual bodies, he said. They also had dark complexions, not the pale white skin made reference to in many journal articles and letters.

Barber believes the vampire myth has its roots in attempts by peasants to explain epidemics and other disasters around them—a theory that's also been suggested by scientists to explain witches.

Undead or Just Dead?

Often, Barber said, peasants would blame these events on a person who had died recently, he said. The peasants believed the person's spirit, instead of resting in peace, was coming back to do harm.

Sometimes, peasants would dig up a body to prove a vampire existed, Barber said. When they opened the grave, natural decomposition processes could have caused the corpse to appear as if it had been feasting on blood. For example, he said, blood can remain in a liquid state in a corpse and naturally be forced out of the lungs and into the mouth. Sometimes, if the grave were in a colder area, the body wouldn't appear to have decomposed at all, which to those examining it, was evidence that supernatural forces were at work.

True folklore descriptions of vampires are actually descriptions of corpses, said Barber, who worked with a pathologist to examine ancient vampire accounts.

"All that was happening is that the bodies were decomposing and the people's fear and beliefs were so strong that they saw vampires," he said. "They felt very helpless in the face of what was happening and they didn't have many answers.

"Vampires made as much sense as anything else in their world."

Vampirism as a Mental Illness

R.E. Hemphill and T. Zabow

Doctors R.E. Hemphill and T. Zabow are senior lecturers in the department of psychiatry at the University of Cape Town in South Africa. In the following article, Hemphill and Zabow present a definition for clinical vampirism. The authors base their definition on their evaluations of three patients, as well as a re-evaluation of the case of John George Haigh, which occurred in England in the 1940s. The authors' argument distinguishes the characteristics of clinical vampirism from the traits of the mythical vampire found in literature and folklore. In addition, they point out that clinical vampirism is a mental illness, which is very different from other mental illnesses. According to Hemphill and Zabow, "vampirists" usually show no outward symptoms that might suggest to others that they are mentally ill. They warn that a diagnosis of clinical vampirism must not be combined with the symptoms of other diseases or disorders, as this might mask the potential severity of the vampirist's actions. Perhaps Hemphill's and Zabow's analysis

R.E. Hemphill and T. Zabow, "Clinical Vampirism: A Presentation of Three Cases and Re-evaluation of Haigh, the 'Acid Bath Murderer,'" *South African Medical Journal*, vol. 63, February 19, 1983, pp. 278–81. Copyright © 1983 by the South African Medical Association. Reproduced by permission.

will encourage the medical profession to view the disorder of clinical vampirism more clearly in an effort to understand its causes and develop some form of treatment.

Vampirism has been reported in the medical literature for more than a century. It was named after the mythical vampire in order to describe the sucking of blood or drinking of blood to satisfy a craving for it. An interest in the dead has also been recorded, so that vampirism has been confused with necrophilia. . . .

The essential characteristics of the vampire was that he drank fresh blood specifically to satisfy a need, also having an abnormal interest in death and the dead. The appropriate clinical substantive for a human who displays these characteristics is 'vampirist', not vampire, which refers to a supernatural creature or to a bat.

The mythical vampire was an evil spirit which, being refused entry into the 'other world' because of unsuitable behaviour in life or neglect of rituals, returned to the grave as a 'revenant' or 'living dead' being. He re-animated his corpse and sustained it with blood sucked from the living during sleep, or by biting the neck and drinking from the wound. A victim thus attacked or a suicide victim was liable to become a vampire. Vampires lived in cemeteries and seldom left their graves except to satisfy their need for blood: the dead were their people. The vampire did not desecrate graves, violate corpses, eat human flesh or have sexual intercourse with the living. He had no real identity and was thought not to cast a shadow or reflect an image in a mirror. The characteristics of a periodic craving for blood, association with the dead and no certain identity are a triad also found in clinical vampirism. . . .

We suggest that compulsive blood-taking, uncertain identity and an abnormal interest in death, as observed in our cases and reported variously by others, are symptoms of the psychopathology of clinical vampirism. Uncertain identity is probably invariable, while an interest in death may not always be evident.

In addition to non-criminal vampirists, we have intensively studied 3 who had been charged with dishonesty and referred for psychiatric assessment because of self-mutilation. We have also re-examined the case of Haigh, 'acid-bath' murderer of 1949, regarding whom there was much inconclusive controversy in psychiatric circles, and propose that he was also a vampirist. We describe these 4 cases in detail, refer to others and discuss clinical vampirism and its implications. . . .

Re-evaluating John George Haigh

John Haigh, the 'acid-bath' murderer, was executed in London on 10 August 1949 at the age of 40. Haigh confessed that between September 1944 and February 1949 he had killed 9 persons, incised their necks and drunk a cupful of blood from each. Six were friends whose property he then acquired by fraud, but the other 3 were unidentified casual strangers. The primary motive for all the murders, he said, was an irresistible urge for blood, and not gain: 'there are so many other ways of making easy money, though illegitimately'. . . .

Haigh was the only child of sound, middle-class parents for whom he showed genuine affection throughout life. His birth, development and health were normal, there were no congenital or blood disorders, and no family history of mental instability. . . .

He enjoyed blood, and from the age of 6 would lick scratches and wound himself to suck it. He pictured and dreamed of people injured and bleeding after railway accidents. Although of the Plymouth Brethren, he was fascinated by Holy Communion and the Crucifixion, and sometimes saw blood pouring from a large crucifix that hung over the altar in the cathedral, while the bleeding figure of Christ would appear in his dreams.

In 1944, when he was 35, blood dripped into his mouth from an accidental scalp wound. That night he dreamed that his, 'mouth was full of blood, which revived the old taste', and knew that he would have to obtain blood. He killed 2 persons that year, 3 in 1945, 3 in 1948 and Mrs Deacon in February 1949. He said 'before each of my killings I had a series of dreams, I saw a forest of crucifixes that changed into green trees dripping with blood . . . which I drank, and once more I awakened with a desire that demanded fulfilment'. . . . 'The dream cycles started early in the week and culminated on Friday' (i.e. the day of the Crucifixion—author's note).

Collecting Blood

In anticipation of having to kill he arranged to have the use of the storeroom of a small factory in Crawley, where he installed non-corrosive metal drums, carboys of sulphuric acid, a pump, tools and protective clothing. He would club or shoot the victim in the head, plug the wound, incise the neck, draw a cupful of blood and 'drink it for 3 to 5 minutes, after which I felt better'. He would put the body in the drum and pump acid over it. The process of dissolution took a few days and he visited the work-shop daily to inspect. If the body had to be dismembered he greased the floor first, so, that the blood would not sink in and he could wash it away. The 'sludge' was poured down the drain and the drum with what did not dissolve, such as plastic articles or dentures, was thrown on the rubbish heap of the factory yard. . . .

Haigh seemed not to realize that he might die or that the disintegrating bodies had once been alive and his friends.

His only regret was that 'being led by an irresistible urge, I was not given to the discovery of the distress this might cause to myself and others', by which he meant his parents and friends. He wrote to his mother from the death cell: 'My spirit will remain earthbound for a while. My mission is not yet fulfilled.' Haigh was unconcerned about his trial and refused to appeal against his sentence. A panel of psychiatrists found that he was not legally insane and that he had no symptoms of mental illness; his electro-encephalogram (EEG) was normal. . . .

The Case Studies

The three unmarried White males described below all came from good middle-class homes with stable, affectionate parents and siblings, and no family psychopathology. Birth and development were normal, and they were well-built, reasonably good-looking and, apart from self-mutilation, physically and mentally healthy and free from congenital defects or blood disorders. In all the central nervous system and EEGs were normal, and their IQs 110–120. All found cannibalism revolting and films about Dracula 'rubbish'. They were not interested in the occult or religion, and had no food fads.

Case Study #1

This 27-year-old had been expelled from 5 schools between the ages of 8 and 13 and thereafter detained in residential schools, reformatories, prisons and a treatment unit, except when he absconded and when released for 7 months at the age of 20 and 3 months at the age of 26. . . .

He was an attractive, wilful child, liable to tantrums, violence and cruelty. From the age of 4 he burned curtains, smashed furniture, bashed his teddy bear against the wall, mutilated his pet birds and chameleons, hanged his dog and cat and terrorized the school.

He was always impulsive, reckless, vindictive and incapable of remorse. Violence, human injuries and blood excited him, but he got no pleasure out of inflicting pain. He relieved frustration in prison by tearing rats apart and indulging in the blood. . . .

From the age of 4 he sucked his blood and later cut himself and opened veins longitudinally for the purpose. From the age of 24 he had dreams of tying a boy to a tree and slashing him. When the blood spouted in his dreams, he wakened 'satisfied and drained'. After such dreams a desire for exogenous blood led him to buy fresh blood at the abattoir [slaughterhouse] and drink it with 'a warm, relaxed feeling, not sexual'. He would bite the neck or shoulder of his partners to suck their blood, and sometimes thought of cutting them with a knife. The craving subsided for several weeks after taking his own or exogenous [outside the body] blood. Blood 'warmed and relaxed' him; alcohol and drugs did not influence the blood interest.

From childhood he dreamed of being dead and kept dead creatures in his room. At the age of 26 he visited cemeteries in the hope of exhuming a fresh body, and longed to have one to 'cherish it'. He never had necrophiliac sexual desires. He would visualize himself as dead and 'longed to have cancer' like his mother so as to experience her suffering 'inside' and her death. He falsely confessed to having murdered a child in the hope of 'seeing what it was like to be hanged', as he believed that only one part of him would die and the other would observe execution. His identity was never certain. He had three separate names and separate prison records; 'I am never sure which I am at any time', he said. . . .

Case Study #2

This 19-year-old had been sent to a reformatory. From the age of 17 he had travelled around the country associating with criminals, living by crime, and indulging heavily in drugs and alcohol. He was grossly psychopathic but had some feeling for his parents. Since childhood he had been prone to tantrums and violence, and was unfeeling, impulsive, vindictive and incapable of remorse. He tormented animals and children and committed arson.

From the age of 16 he had stabbed strangers on impulse, 'some of whom may have died'. He enjoyed burning shops, robbing, smashing windows and stealing cars during political riots. Recurrent dreams of violence, blood and mutilated people 'gave him peace'. He had no real interest in sex and feared he might kill a sexual partner.

As regards blood he said: 'I have liked the appearance and taste of blood all my life. I would lick scratches and cut myself for it. I used to pull off birds' heads and drink their blood, I bit the head off a guinea pig when I was a child and sucked the blood, and pulled off the head of a chicken, collected the blood in my hands and drank it. I cut myself in order to get blood. Blood relaxes me. I think if I got it every few days, I would be settled. When I feel annoyed, the sight of blood usually calms me, but if it does not, I smash my fists against the wall and lick the blood, even tear my clothes up. It is the feeling of blood in me not the taste that I need, I would like to get it from another person, but so far have not worked out how.'

From about the age of 6 he had kept dead animals in his room and talked to the dead in the graveyard. He still envied them, and asked 'are they as unhappy as I am?' He never knew who he really was: 'I can't understand myself, so how could other people understand me?' In order to attain an identity he joined the Cape Scorpions, an exclusive criminal gang, and was tattooed with their emblem, but never identified with them. . . .

Case Study #3

This 22-year-old broke his arm at the age of 5, and at the age of 8 smashed his right knee with loss of patella and tissue, in road accidents. He enjoyed hospital and picked off the skin grafts in order both to prolong his stay and suck blood. From the age of 13 he mutilated himself in other ways, was hospitalized many times and, to date, has received many blood transfusions when exsanguinated and more than 200 anaesthetics. . . .

He said: 'I have never been upset by the sight of blood, but enjoyed it tremendously. When I was young it was a habit to suck blood, which soon became a craving and I had to have it. I cut myself to get blood, but as I dislike pain, I usually get it by scraping the granulations which does not hurt much, collecting a cupful and drinking it. I get the craving frequently. I cannot say what sets it off. I have always liked the taste of blood, but it is the feeling of having it inside me that is important, and a transfusion is more satisfying than drinking it . . . I was always fascinated by death and from the age of 4 visited cemeteries, hoping to see bodies and bones.'

He enjoyed surgical and accident wards, seeing the sick and dying, helping nurses with patients' dressings and watching blood transfusions. He asked, unsuccessfully, to work in the mortuary and postmortem rooms. He mutilated himself for blood and to get back into hospital. 'Blood, sickness and death are all connected in some ways. I would love to be dead. I would love to have the experience of death. I would really love it. I have no real idea who I am, I am often scared of what, whoever I am, might do.' He only felt real in a hospital. For a few weeks after leaving he was free from unreal feelings and the desire for blood. He rapidly became unsettled, injured himself and was urgently admitted to a hospital. While he was under observation in this hospital he was quiet and unsociable. He managed to cut himself or scrape his wound occasionally to suck blood. During the few years since his discharge he has continued to injure himself very severely.

Analyzing the Data

These 4 subjects each displayed the triad of vampirism. They ingested their own and exogenous blood from victims (Haigh), partners and abattoirs (case 1), animals and clinical specimens (case 2), and blood transfusions (case 3). They frequently dreamed of bloodshed and death.

Death attracted them, not as a release from suffering but because they wished to 'experience it' as 'living dead' in the company of the dead. . . .

In one way or another all expressed a belief that in dying they would achieve another, more real existence.

Their identities were changeable and uncertain. . . .

All had satisfactory family, medical and psychiatric histories. Vampirism and psychopathy developed in spite of favourable influences and no possible causes for either were discovered. The patients were disinterested in sex, and blood evoked no sexual feeling. . . .

Mental unrest and an increasing desire for blood preceded each indulgence. Recurrent blood dreams sometimes dramatized the urgency, and Haigh said he would have to kill for blood shortly after a significant dream. The visions of bleeding forests and crucifixes of Haigh and case 1, and the latter's drawing of a blood demon must have had a similar origin in their unconscious.

Taking a taste or a cupful of blood was followed by a warm, relaxed feeling, with calm and disappearance of the craving. This lasted from 1 day to months, perhaps longer. It is not known whether Haigh took his own blood between murders. The indulgence was neither a habit nor an addiction. Vampirism is a rare compulsive disorder with an irresistible urge for blood ingestion, a ritual necessary to bring mental relief; like other compulsions, its meaning is not understood by the participant.

Theories of Vampirism

Any theory about vampirism is speculative. What we propose assumes the unconscious persistence of ancient myths. In mythology blood contained the essence and qualities of the host which could be transferred to another. Thus a victor drank the blood of his enemy in order to possess his powers, and a vampire sucked blood from the living in order to obtain regeneration.

Archaic man's fear of a blood-sucking spirit and of becoming a 'revenant' became an archetypal myth from which human vampirism evolved. The human vampirist is analogous to the vampire, with the common features of the main triad and unease, isolation and the 'mirror defect'. The activities of the human vampirist throughout the ages may have given real substance to the belief in the vampire and reinforced the myth. Vampirism today is therefore a rare atavism [the reappearance or reoccurrence of a particular trait or characteristic] and blood-taking a ritual act of regeneration.

Frequency of Clinical Vampirism

How common is vampirism? A few cases of probable vampirism have been published, such as Krafft-Ebing's case No. 31 who paid to prick women and suck their blood, McCully' case who from the age of 13 periodically cut his neck and caught the blood in his mouth, and tried unsuccessfully to involve another boy, and Bourguignon's female patient who repeatedly sucked blood from a pharyngeal angioma, later bleeding to death. . . .

Vampirism seems to vary in frequency and intensity,

from our fully developed cases to the disturbed young women who occasionally cut themselves to taste their blood. Nothing is known about remission or permanent resolution; there is no specific treatment.

Since vampirism involves unprovoked violence against the subject or another person it might be regarded as a variant of sadomasochism; there is insufficient evidence to show whether this may be the case. In vampirism the specific motive is to obtain and ingest blood, and not indulgence in cruelty, self-punishment or self-degradation, and therefore in our view it is not essentially sadomasochistic and is a clinical entity.

Although rare, vampirism has serious clinical and practical implications. Male auto-vampirists may attack others for blood; both males and females are a recurrent treatment problem. Self-mutilation is not rare among violent recidivist prisoners, some of whom may be vampirists. The circumstances, motives and blood interest of criminals who mutilate themselves, or who have scars from repeated self-mutilation, should be inquired into carefully. Old and recent scars, together with puncture wounds convenient for sucking blood, are very suspicious.

Vampirism is thus a possible cause of unpredictable repeated murder which is likely to be overlooked.

The vampirist may show no obvious signs of mental disorder. It is a disturbing thought that a pleasant person, like Haigh, unsuspected, may be a vampirist liable to a period craving for blood.

Porphyria Is Real, Vampires Are Not

Norine Dresser

As a folklorist, Norine Dresser is particularly skilled at sifting through cultural artifacts and events in search of the truth behind many of our traditional stories and myths. In *American Vampires*, Dresser seeks to uncover the truth about vampires and to determine why we are so fascinated by them. Ultimately, Dresser concludes that vampires are figures of folklore and myth, purely fiction. However, their image has the power to inflict great pain and suffering all the same. In the following excerpt, Dresser presents the story of Dr. David Dolphin and his remarkable vampire hypothesis. Speaking at a professional medical conference in 1985, Dr. Dolphin claimed that vampirism could be explained. He argued that people who drink blood suffer from a rare disease called porphyria. Dolphin's statement incited a media frenzy that basically labeled porphyria sufferers as direct descendants from Count Dracula. To clear up the misinformation spread by Dr. Dolphin and the media, Dresser carefully defines porphyria and explains its symptoms. Her work illustrates how quickly fact and fiction can merge to create a story that, while having very little basis in reality, can still have a very significant impact on our culture—much like the traditional vampire myth. An important question related to the mystery of vampires and determining whether or not they exist in our modern world is suggested by Dresser's sensitive exploration of porphyria: If a poorly researched hypothesis can provoke such media frenzy, public outcry, tale-telling, superstition, and rampant misinformation in the twentieth century, what might such prejudicial labeling or mass hysteria have done to perpetuate the image of the vampire in the Middle Ages?

On May 30, 1985, David Dolphin, Ph.D., professor of chemistry at the University of British Columbia, gave a startling presentation to the American Association for the Advancement of Science. He hypothesized that blood-drinking vampires were, in fact, victims of porphyria, an incurable genetic disease affecting at least 50,000 patients in the United States that causes sudden symptoms of severe pain, respiratory problems, skin lesions, and sometimes death. He suggested that some of the symptoms could be alleviated by an injection of heme (the pigmented component of hemoglobin and related substances, found in largest amounts in the bone marrow, red blood cells, and the liver). Dolphin announced, "Since in the Middle Ages an injection of the red pigment of blood would not be possible, what else might take its place? If a large amount of blood were to be drunk then the heme in it, if it passes through the stomach wall to the bloodstream, would serve the same purpose." He declared, "It is our contention tha blood drinking vampires were in fact victims of porphyria trying to alleviate the symptoms of their dreadful disease."

Symptoms Linked to Vampires

Dolphin described the photosensitivity of porphyria victims, stating that the effects of exposure to even mild sunlight could be devastating. To him this would be consistent with the folklore concerning the nocturnal behavior of vampires. He spoke of "lesions of the skin being so severe that the nose and fingers could be destroyed." He discussed hairiness, pigmentation, and depigmentation. He indicated that while the teeth became no larger, lips and gums became taut so that the teeth appeared to be much more prominent. . . .

Dr. Dolphin expanded on his hypothesis, suggesting that chemical reactions to garlic by porphyria patients were such that garlic might increase the severity of a porphyria attack, and thus might well act to keep vampires away because they would want to avoid any substance that aggravated their condition. According to his view, this negative effect of garlic occurs because its principal constituent is dialkyl disulfide, which destroys heme. This can set off a reaction increasing the severity of a porphyria attack.

Dolphin also addressed the issue of the incidence of the disease. He tried to correlate the folklore of the vampire's bite, causing the victim to become a vampire, with the genetic pattern of porphyria. He explained that while siblings may share the same defective gene from this generally autosomal dominant trait (inherited from one parent), sometimes only one sibling will display symptoms. However, he noted that a strain on the system from an excess of drugs, alcohol, or sudden loss of a large quantity of blood could trigger the disease in a person genetically predisposed. . . .

Professional societies like the American Association for he Advancement of Science annually hold meetings where scholars, like Dr. Dolphin, present new theoretical concepts for peers to debate and criticize. Professional meetings are created as a forum for the examination and evaluation of new concepts, as well as for reconsideration of older, well-accepted theories. . . .

On the other hand, the media have different objectives. Their goal is to grab the attention of the public with eye- and ear-catching topics in order to transmit information as quickly and widely as possible. So it is that newspaper and wire services across the country seized upon Dolphin's presentation. The result was front-page feature stories, often accompanied by pictures of Lon Chaney or Bela Lugosi about to sink his teeth into the neck of a beautiful young female victim. The *Washington Post* trumpeted its story with "Dracula Wolf Man Legends May Contain a Drop of Truth: Genetic Disorder May Trigger Thirst for Blood." *Newsweek* proclaimed, "Vampire Diagnosis: Real Sick." The *Sacramento Bee* heralded, "Bad Blood Takes Bite Out of Vampire Myth." As far away as Poland, headlines announced, "Did Vampires Exist in Reality?—They Are Simply Porphyria Patients"; "Did Vampires and Werewolves Exist in the Real World?"; and "Vampires Are Simply People Sick on Porphyria.". . .

What the media failed to consider was how the 50,000 incurable porphyria patients would be affected when they promoted Professor Dolphin's hypothesis of a biochemical basis to ancient and feared beliefs about legendary entities.

The Truth About Porphyria

According to the American Porphyria Foundation, whose board is composed of physicians with fifteen to twenty years' experience in the field, porphyria is not one disease, but a constellation of seven different inheritable diseases, some of which are life threatening. It is so rare as to be classified an "orphan disease"—a label applied to any disord that affects fewer than 200,000 people. It is often a silent disease, meaning that the gene for it can be carried and passed on to others without ever causing any problems.

Porphyria is a metabolic disorder caused by a deficiency in an enzyme involved with the synthesis of heme. Each of the forms has its own symptomatology and treatment. For example, patients with acute intermittent porphyria (AIP) have no photosensitivity problems, but require injections of heme during severe bouts of pain. It is particularly dangerous if the diagnosis has not been made and if harmful drugs are administered. Although symptoms generally resolve following an attack, some patients develop chronic pain.

The symptoms often seem mysterious, appearing suddenly. They can include rapid onset of muscle paralysis in arms and legs, seizures, confusion, headaches, agitation, blindness, tachycardia (rapid heartbeat), and constant vomiting. Chemical imbalances can cause mental problems, such as hallucinations. In acute cases, respiratory failure and death result.

In contrast, patients with porphyria cutania tarda (PCT), the most common form, have skin problems, typically fragility and blistering of areas exposed to sunlight. There may be an over-abundance or lack of pigmentation and excess facial hair. . . .

The most extreme and rare form is congenital erythropoietic porphyria (CEP), also known as Gunther's disease. It usually manifests during childhood. Skin photosensitivity may be extreme and lead to blistering, severe scarring, and increased hair growth. Removal of the spleen and blood transfusions are treatment possibilities.

Blood transfusions are used to suppress the patient's own marrow because it is here that the porphyrins are produced. Porphyrins are a natural product of the body, pumped out the bone marrow, but if they are produced at excessive rates, then symptoms of porphyria occur. Blood transfusions can shut down the body's abnormal porphyrin production.

CEP is the only form of the disease with even a remote possibility of correlation with the vampire's supposed physical characteristics, for here there may be hairiness, mutilation affecting the nose, shortened fingers or loss of the ends of the fingers and possibly pointed teeth. However, the hypothesis could not apply even here because blood taken by mouth supposedly to counter the heme deficiency, cannot reach the blood in the circulation system, It would be broken down in the gut to iron and amino acids, which have no effect on any form of porphyria. . . .

Porphyria Is No Joke

As is apparent, to have porphyria is no laughing matter. Yet porphyria patients immediately became the targets of jokes and victims of avoidance, fear, and derision as a result of the publicity blitz ignited by the hypothesis. The association of the relatively unknown porphyria with the very well known vampire set off a chain reaction of unexpected and unpleasant events because the allure of the vampire is so strong in this country.

Desiree (Dee) Dodson, director of the American Porphyria Foundation, reported that phone and mail contacts increased 500 percent. She described it as a "nightmare" because she could not keep up with all the mail and was barraged with phone calls from incensed patients all over the country. . . .

A porphyria patient who runs a hotline for sufferers in New England complained that she was very angry with her local paper's headline about the "Vampire Disease.". . .

This woman described two panic-stricken couples, each of whom was being driven apart by the publicity. In both cases the wives had the disease and the husbands could not deal with it. According to this informant, both women were newly diagnosed. Before the publicity, porphyria had been an unknown, but afterward the attitude of each of the husbands was "I don't know if I can handle this or if I want to live with this person. I don't know if I even want to talk to you" [the person running the hotline]. These husbands were horrified by the notion that they might be married to vampires. Their emotional responses blurred their logic. They began to consider that maybe the vampire was something real. . . .

Medical Opinions of Dolphin's Hypothesis

There are approximately only forty porphyria specialists in the United States. Some of them reported that their patients were able to handle the publicity fairly well, being more amused than angry. However, publicly and in private correspondence, most of the scientific community has not supported the porphyria hypothesis. In a *New York Times* headline in the Letters to the Editor section, "Vampire Label Unfair to Porphyria Sufferers," porphyria specialist Dr. Claus A. Pierach of Abbott Northwestern Hospital in Minneapolis, Minnesota, expressed his concern. He charged that the idea of porphyria patients having something in common with werewolves or vampires was too "far-fetched.". . .

He concluded, "It was irresponsible to perpetuate the myth linking porphyria with fairy tales. Our many patients lead normal lives and deserve no such blemish." However, in a later response to my inquiry he wrote that something good might come out of all the "hoopla," bringing more attention to the disease and the porphyria patients closer together.

D. Montgomery Bissell, M.D., a porphyria specialist and researcher at the University of California at San Francisco, summarizes the medical objections to the porphyria hypothesis. He points out that Dolphin's remarks did not address any of the various forms of porphyria; that no patients have a craving for blood, and that blood given by mouth to persons with heme-deficient porphyria (CEP or AIP) is useless. Dr. Bissell declared that even transfused blood would likely have little effect. Instead, what these people need is a chemical called hematin, which is extracted from blood. Finally, he refuted the concept that a sudden loss of a lot of blood could trigger the disease in someone genetically predisposed. Bissell explained that the heme-deficient porphyrias involve the liver and not the bone marrow, and that blood loss has no effect on liver heme metabolism. For this reason acute attacks of porphyria cannot be induced by blood loss.

Dr. Karl Anderson of New York Medical College in Valhalla, New York, stated that CEP (the rarest form of the disease and the one that comes closest to fitting the scheme) could not have given rise to vampire stories because no one in the Middle Ages knew that its victims had a blood deficiency. He emphasized that these victims do not develop a thirst for blood. . . .

Hypothesis Lacks Supporting Evidence

The only form of porphyria which has the symptoms of photosensitivity, hairiness, pointy teeth, *and* a need for additional blood is CEP, the rarest form. Since there have been only sixty cases reported in the world, it is highly unlikely that the rarest form of a disease, which occurs so infrequently (less than 5 percent of carriers have attacks), could have served as the origin of such a widespread myth. . . .

Since Dr. Dolphin stated that he was talking about people in the Middle Ages, it is necessary to look to the accounts from the past to see if his associations hold up. For example, he refers to the photosensitivity and subsequent pallor of porphyria patients, who must avoid the sunlight

This may correspond to Stoker's creative writing and white-faced movie versions of vampires, but it does not necessarily pertain to the early folklore about the vampire. . . . [T]he bodies of persons accused of being vampires in those times that were exhumed were described as being dark, black, or ruddy in color, and never with pallor.

Other points from folklore which diverge from the hypothesis include Dolphin's citing of pointed teeth as evidence of commonality. Actually, possessing fangs and being long of tooth are other parts of the Stoker book and the movie image and are not found in references from earlier times. . . . [I]t was the tongue, rather than the teeth, that was thought to be the tool of attack.

In contrast, today fangs have become a hallmark of vampire descriptions. John Vellutini, editor of the *Journal of Vampirology* and a critic of the porphyria hypothesis, states that in contemporary folklore vampire teeth are usually described as shining or gleaming, "terms hardly suggestive of discoloration." Yet tooth discoloration, caused by very high levels of porphyrins, is what happens to porphyria patients with CEP—again, the only form that even comes close to matching Dolphin's ideas.

A further relationship which Dolphin tries to establish is the incidence of the disease with the incidence of vampire folklore. He refers to isolated pockets of small, intermarrying populations. As an example, he cites Transylvania. Transylvania was the geographical place selected by Stoker for his creative exposition and is not known as a center for vampire beliefs. Rather, vampire beliefs have been recorded from all over the world and are not confined to isolated geographical locations. The limited distribution of porphyria does not match the widespread phenomenon of vampire stories and beliefs.

Vellutini proposes another criticism. "The attributing of

photosensitivity to the legendary vampire represents personal speculation rather than folklore." He points out that
the notion of the vampire restricting its activities to the
night is a common and contemporary misconception. He
gives several examples from Greek beliefs indicating that
vampires appeared in full daylight, even at noon. . . .

By now it should be clear that the porphyria/vampire hypothesis has not been supported by the medical community, which works directly with porphyria patients. . . .

It is apparent that the Dolphin hypothesis is more tied to
the concept of vampires as conceived by Bram Stoker, per-
sonified by Count Dracula, and embellished by movie versions, particularly as embodied by Bela Lugosi. Stoker's
Count Dracula is fiction. Vampires are a fiction—one we
have all absorbed.

Epilogue: Analyzing the Evidence

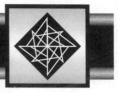

"There are such mysteries which men can only guess at, which age by age, they may solve only in part."
    —Dr. Abraham Van Helsing, in Bram Stoker's *Dracula*

Do such creatures as vampires really exist? Or are they simply a fiction created by the human imagination as a way to deal with irrational fears? The evidence presented in this book suggests that there is no easy answer to this question. It may no longer be possible to look at the question of whether vampires exist from either a purely superstitious point of view or from the viewpoint of literature, folklore, and mythology. The answer to the mystery of the vampire is not so black and white, and the question of the vampire's existence cannot be answered with a simple yes or no.

Developing a Critical Perspective

Your job is to evaluate the evidence presented in this book and question how the authors reached their conclusions. Then you can decide whether the evidence presented helps you to determine whether vampires exist. In order to evaluate the evidence effectively, you must examine it from a critical perspective. This means that you must look carefully at the author's work, the evidence presented, the way he or she argues the points, and his or her conclusions. To do this, first question the writing and break the argument down into several parts. You can then look more closely at these parts and determine whether the author's argument is based on research and objective analysis or if it is simply based on assumptions and uninformed opinions. Finding out if the evidence the author presents is reliable will help you to decide whether it is possible for vampires to exist.

Why is it important to examine the pieces in this book—or anything else for that matter—from a critical perspective? Doing so will enable you to become a better thinker. And developing sound critical thinking skills will enable you to think for yourself rather than letting others tell you what to think. Many of us accept the information we are given every day at face value, often believing it just because someone who is an "expert" or an authority figure tells us that we should. The authors whose work is collected in this book might be considered experts on vampires. Through their work, they try to discover and present the truth about whether vampires exist. However, simply putting together evidence, or reasons, for or against the existence of vampires does not mean that their conclusions are necessarily correct. You see examples of this in your everyday life, particularly in political ad campaigns. A candidate compiles reasons why you should not vote for her opponent and should vote for her instead; however, the evidence the candidate compiles for herself and against her opponent is often unreliable or misrepresented. Developing solid critical thinking skills will allow you to examine things more deeply through questioning and evaluation. For example, instead of just believing that vampires do not exist because several authors in this book have told you that they do not, you will use critical thinking skills to question and evaluate what they are saying. This will allow you to come to your own conclusions about what you should believe about vampires and why.

Thinking critically about a subject involves questioning and evaluating the topic objectively. This means that you do not think about it according to your feelings on the subject; rather, you focus only on the evidence or facts as they a* presented, how well they are presented, and whether t⸺

are reliable. By carefully evaluating and questioning the evidence, it is possible to arrive at some form of truth, or at least to find an answer to your questions about vampires. The ability to think critically takes lots of practice. This essay is designed to introduce you to several critical thinking strategies that will enable you to effectively evaluate the authors' evidence and arguments about whether vampires are fact or fiction.

Critical Thinking Strategies and Goals

Your goal as a critical thinker is to determine whether the evidence presented to you about vampires is reliable and well informed. You should know that reliable evidence will be presented to you objectively and will not be based on the writer's particular feelings about vampires. You will first have to determine if the evidence is based on accurate research and information (generally reliable) or if it is based on uninformed opinions and personal feelings (usually unreliable). Valid opinions may be informed through research, experience, or specialized expertise in a field. But opinions may also be uninformed, meaning that they are not verifiable through experience or expertise but exist simply because the author wishes to hold them for convenience or because they correspond with his own values and beliefs. Even though evidence may be presented in a convincing way, you do not have to accept it as fact.

To illustrate and practice the critical thinking techniques you will use in evaluating the evidence presented in this book, let's examine two articles. "Grave Discoveries," by Manuella Dunn Mascetti, contains evidence that supports the existence of vampires. Another selection, "Vampires and the Facts of Decomposition," by Paul Barber, presents evidence arguing against the existence of vampires. The critical thinking process involves five steps. These steps will explain in detail what is involved in working through the strategy and demonstrate how to apply the strategy to the above articles.

Step One: Examining the Author's Credentials and Background

The first step in evaluating the evidence by Barber and Mascetti is to examine their credentials, or their background and experience. What qualifications do they possess that make it important for you to consider their claims and evidence as valid? This step is important for two reasons. The first is that in order to form a solid conclusion of your own, you want to have the best evidence at your disposal. The best evidence is most likely to be presented by authors who have done adequate research on the topic, who themselves demonstrate an ability to think critically about the issue, and who perhaps have some expertise in studying vampires that goes beyond their opinions and beliefs. Evidence presented by authors with these qualifications is considered to be more valuable and worthy of consideration.

However, even these qualifications do not make the evidence presented either for or against the existence of vampires absolutely certain. This leads us to the second important reason for examining an author's credentials. The fact is that even experts can be wrong, or later proven to have been wrong, based on new or more current research. You might need to determine if the information these authors are providing to you is correct and has not been proven wrong by new research in the field of vampire studies. If they are truly experts in their field, they will take very seriously their responsibility to present the most up-to-date research on the topic.

With this in mind, what can you tell about Barber and Mascetti and whether the evidence they present regarding the existence of vampires is worth consideration? What do the background and experience tell you about the potential reliability of the arguments they have written? In the biographical introduction to Mascetti's piece, you are told that she has done a great deal of research on mythological subjects. Many people consider vampires to be a mythological subject. You might be inclined to accept her as an expert based on the fact that she has researched and published previously, though this does not mean that her research is necessarily well done or even accurate. She simply meets some of the important professional criteria. In addition to her writing experience, Mascetti uses a famous eyewitness account of a vampire attack that has not only been written down but was also authorized and verified by military personnel at the scene. This account serves as the primary source of evidence for her argument and indicates that she understands the importance of having strong evidence available to her readers. Her credentials indicate that her work is worthy of consideration.

The credentials of the other author, Paul Barber, are also impressive. His introductory biography tells you that he is the author of a book on vampires and burial practices and also that he has done work on both folklore (which is generally believed to be fiction) and reality as they relate to the subject of vampires. Since it is your goal to examine the mystery of vampires in relation to whether they are fact or fiction, Barber's credentials already indicate that his work could be helpful to you. Barber is also listed as a research associate at a major California university, which indicates that he likely has the expertise necessary to conduct thorough research on a variety of topics. His job gives his writing further credibility. Overall, Barber's background and experience make his work important to consider in your search for answers to the mystery of the vampire's existence.

To practice the steps of developing a critical perspective in evaluating evidence, it is only necessary for us to examine the works of these two selected authors. However, you might be asked at some time to evaluate the work of several authors, selecting the best three pieces from six authors, for example. In this situation, it becomes even more important for you to examine the background and credentials of the authors you select. If you must choose the best evidence to support your argument, you will want it to come from the most reliable sources. We have discussed the credentials of two of the twelve authors in this book and have found them both to be worth considering for this exercise. But if you were asked to choose between Barber and Mascetti, which would you think had the most reliable credentials, and why? Who appears to be more of an expert? Do you think the piece by the author with more expertise will automatically be the best one? Or might the piece by the author with less expertise be just as successful? These are important questions to ask yourself as you evaluate the work of the authors in this book. Each author whose work is included in this book was chosen because he or she had something to offer the argument about whether vampires exist. Remember, although credentials and experience are important, experts can sometimes be wrong or misinformed. Your job is to ask appropriate questions and think critically about the background of these experts.

Step Two: Determining the Author's Hypothesis or Claim

A hypothesis, or claim, is a statement concerning the main idea or point the author is trying to prove in his writing. Each author in this book presents evidence in support of one of two hypotheses: either that vampires are real or that vampires are a fiction. An author uses a hypothesis as a way to explain the series of facts or evidence he will use to prove his hypothesis about vampires is the correct one. The fa and evidence supporting the author's claims can then be tested for accuracy by further investigation or research.

How does the hypothesis work in practice? Based on experience or research, an author may hypothesize that vampires are real. The author's questions or ideas about vampires will guide his or her further research. The author will look for information that will support his or her hypothesis or answer his or her questions concerning vampires. The author will then present this research in an effort to convince others that his or her hypothesis is correct. Others may disagree with the author's hypothesis that vampires are real and go about using the same process to prove their hypothesis that vampires do not exist.

It is important to identify the author's hypothesis so that you can determine whether the evidence he or she uses to support it is strong and valid or weak and questionable. In addition, if the author's hypothesis is not clear, you may conclude that the evidence he or she presents may also be weak or unclear. In this case, it may not be worthwhile for you to consider the article. The hypothesis should be clearly stated and provable. However, not all hypotheses are proven successfully. Although an author may make an attempt to prove the hypothesis, it can fail due to inadequate research or the author's reliance on his or her own opinions instead of reliable evidence.

The author's claim can usually be clearly stated in one or two sentences, but it may be longer and more complex in the piece you are examining. You need to synthesize the author's information and restate his or her hypothesis clearly and simply in your own words. In some cases, the author may have more than one hypothesis in a single article. Each of these must be looked at separately in order to think critically about the entire article. Let's take a look at Mascetti's and Barber's hypotheses and discuss each one in detail.

Mascetti's hypothesis: Since the common perception of the vampire is based on a fictional image, the information available through eyewitness accounts is valuable in determining what real vampires look like and how they behave. Mascetti's piece is offered as one that provides evidence that vampires exist. She relies heavily on a well-known documented eyewitness account of the vampire Peter Plogojowitz as proof that vampires exist. Mascetti claims that the real vampires described in eyewitness accounts, the story of Peter Plogojowitz being just one example, look very different than the vampire familiar in books and movies. She hypothesizes that a careful examination of the authentic eyewitness reports of vampires will help to separate the fact from the fiction in order to better understand and identify the vampire in whatever shape it may take. You will expect the evidence she provides to support this hypothesis.

Barber's hypothesis: Eyewitness accounts of vampires can be explained using scientific and psychological research. Barber's piece argues the opposite viewpoint: Vampires do not exist. He hypothesizes that eyewitness accounts of vampires can be explained by developing a greater understanding of the power of dreams to shape people's belief systems as well as studying the natural decomposition processes of human corpses. Barber's hypothesis concludes that vampires are imaginary creatures that are the result of superstitions and incorrect assumptions. Barber's job is to convince you that his hypothesis is correct by providing evidence to support it.

Step Three: Evaluating the Evidence

Evidence is used to support the hypothesis of the author. Before we examine the types of evidence used by Mascetti and Barber, it would be helpful to discuss briefly the different types of evidence available. The authors whose work appears in this book use the following types of evidence:

Personal experience. Evidence based on personal experience is not necessarily the most reliable form of evidence, but it is the most widely available. The problem with evidence based on personal experience is that it can be colored by subjectivity, or one's feelings, values, and biases about a particular person, place, or thing.

Published reports. This form of evidence is usually one of the more reputable types, but it is still far from perfect. Evidence from published reports can be found from a wide variety of sources—basically anything in print, from encyclopedias to scholarly journals, from books to magazines. When considering evidence from published reports, quality is key. Research must be thorough and well documented. Statements must be clear and effective. Facts must not be confused with opinions.

Unpublished reports. Using this type of evidence is very risky since it is hard to confirm whether it is true. Unpublished reports may be gossipy in nature or may just be secondhand information that could have gotten skewed in the translation from person to person.

Eyewitness testimony. This type of evidence relies on the words of individuals who witnessed an event. It is usually considered highly reliable; however, it shares some of the same problems with personal experience and unpublished reports. Since it is based on an individual's perception of events and can be influenced by any number of factors, such as fear or environment, it is a very subjective form of evidence. This means it is often colored by emotions or other factors that could cause the witness to perceive things inaccurately.

Expert opinion. Although not all opinions are considered to be objective, expert opinion is considered to be the most reliable form of evidence. Evidence based on the opinion of an expert may be informed by personal experience, but it is usually confirmed and validated based on research and professional expertise.

Experimental evidence. Experimental evidence can happen in two locations. In the laboratory, the researcher can control and change the environmental and physical conditions of the experiment. Experiments in the field, though they have the benefit of occurring in a natural setting, can still be influenced by the researcher's presence or by conditions he or she introduces. When considering this type of evidence, you need to ask how much of the results were influenced intentionally by the researcher to get the desired effect and what would have happened if the researcher had not interfered.

Formal observation. Like experimental evidence, there are two types of observational research. One is called detached observation, in which the researcher simply puts himself in the environment to observe and document what is happening. In participatory observation, the researcher will actually include himself in the event being observed. In both cases, the position of the researcher in relation to the events being observed can influence the final outcome. In both types of observation, the researcher may analyze and draw conclusions about his documentation.

Research review. This type of evidence is used by several of the authors in this book. It is less common since it is used only by writers who have access to a large body of research on a particular topic. This type of evidence involves reading all of the academic research on a topic. The author evaluates the findings and identifies the key points, recurring themes, or major controversies in the subject. He or she then summarizes all of the evidence for the reader. This approach to handling a large amount of evidence is effective, but it has some problems. The author evaluating the evidence may have a hard time keeping his or her own personal values, biases, and beliefs out of the evaluation. Or the author may accidentally even intentionally, leave out some portions of evidence that he or she does not agree with or finds problematic. Although this is an ideal way to make a great deal of information available to many people, it is also difficult for the author to report fairly and accurately all he or she has examined.

The most important thing to remember when examining and evaluating evidence is that it needs to show you, rather than tell you, that the author's hypothesis is valid. The evidence Mascetti and Barber use to support their hypotheses must clearly show why their hypotheses are correct or valid. The evidence either in support of vampires or against them is designed to show you that the author has proof that what he or she thinks about vampires is logical. The author should not simply state his or her opinion that vampires exist, for example. The author's opinion is no better than anyone else's. What you are looking for is whether the author can prove, or show you, that his or her opinion is valid based on some research or evidence. This would then demonstrate that the hypothesis is possible and should be considered worthwhile. Now that you are familiar with some of the different types of evidence authors use, we will examine the work of both Mascetti and Barber and the ways in which they use evidence to support their hypotheses about the existence of vampires.

Examining the Evidence Offered by Mascetti

Mascetti's hypothesis. Since the common perception of the vampire is based on a fictional image, the information available through eyewitness accounts is valuable in determining what real vampires look like and how they behave. In order to support her hypothesis, Mascetti uses only one form of evidence, the eyewitness account. In the excerpt provided, she uses the single account of the vampire Peter Plogojowitz as proof that vampires exist. She then analyzes the key points in the account to determine whether what the villagers saw was in fact a "genuine case of vampirism." She concludes, based on her analysis, that Plogojowitz was in fact a vampire, and she uses his habits and characteristics as a way to define and identify a real vampire.

Mascetti's choice of this eyewitness account is noteworthy. It is not the account of a single witness; rather, it is an official military compilation of events witnessed by several townspeople, along with medical and military officials. Since the events can be corroborated by more than one person, this piece of eyewitness evidence has a greater degree of reliability. However, we cannot forget that Mascetti's evidence is still subjective, that it is a retelling of the personal experience of the witnesses and that it carries with it their own beliefs, fears, and perceptions. These perceptions, although valid, are not necessarily based on fact. When considering Mascetti's evidence and its reliability, you might ask yourself if there is any way to verify that these events really happened. The piece used by Mascetti is an account compiled by one writer based on what several people claim to have seen. Is it possible to locate documentation from the other witnesses to this vampire attack? Are there other eyewitness accounts of vampires in this area, or in other areas, that present similar events and characteristics that can be used to strengthen Mascetti's account? Are there any other types of evidence that would help to verify the truth behind this vampire sighting? Does Mascetti acknowledge the source for this account? Where did it come from, and how do you know it really happened? These are the types of questions you need to ask yourself when evaluating the evidence of eyewitnesses.

Even though you may question the reliability of the eyewitness account Mascetti presents, you must also ask yourself if the evidence she provides adequately supports her hypothesis. Mascetti includes the whole text of the eyewitness account at the very beginning of her piece. At the end of it, after some brief commentary, she leads the reader through a very detailed analysis of the key points presented in the eyewitness account in an effort to determine some of the recurrent patterns of vampirism. This detailed analysis allows her to draw several very specific conclusions that define and identify the characteristics of the real vampires seen in eyewitness accounts, which is the more specific goal of her hypothesis. The eyewitness account provides Mascetti with the detailed information she needs to complete her analysis and draw conclusions. Even without any other evidence, the single eyewitness account allows her to accomplish her purpose and thus supports her hypothesis.

Examining the Evidence Offered by Barber

Barber's hypothesis. Eyewitness accounts of vampires can be explained using scientific and psychological research. In contrast to Mascetti, Barber uses various types of evidence to support his hypothesis, among them eyewitness accounts, published reports (though he provides few sources for these), expert opinion (most notably his own since he has spent his career studying this subject), and research review (he evaluates and summarizes many years of research in the field from a vast number of sources). He echoes Mascetti when he writes that what the vampire eyewitnesses saw was very unlike the more common image of the vampire from fiction and film. This actually lends some additional credibility to Mascetti's evaluation of the account. But Barber quickly moves beyond this point to announce that recent findings in forensic pathology (the study of what happens to the body after death) can provide rational explanations for the vampires people claimed to have seen in the eyewitness accounts. As evidence, Barber refers to another equally famous eyewitness account, that of Arnold Paole, which he retells in his own words, describing in detail what eyewitnesses claim to have seen. He then goes on to provide a scientific explanation for each vampiric trait or symptom. For example, the blood often found in the mouth of a dead person suspected of being a vampire did not come from drinking the blood of his or her victims but rather is blood that occurs naturally in a corpse due to a buildup of gases in the body that forces blood up through the lungs and into the mouth.

Using research on the psychology of dreams, Barber continues to demystify the vampire. He explains that vampires who were seen by eyewitnesses prowling around graveyards and outside of windows at night were really the result of dreams had by eyewitnesses based on their own needs or fears. Finally, Barber discusses the very real fear of mass epidemics of disease or contagion due to plague. He argues that the reason people believed that vampires stole people's lives in a short period of time was due to the high probability of disease and contagion they lived with on a daily basis.

Overall, Barber provides a massive amount of evidence to support his hypothesis. Added to his professional credentials, you may have little doubt as to the accuracy and truth behind his research. However, thinking critically about the evidence Barber provides yields some questions. For instance, how accurate is Barber's interpretation of the research he presents? Since he relies heavily on research review as his main source of evidence, you are forced to rely on his interpretation of the research for your information. Since he does not provide source information, except for several works from which he quotes directly, you have no way of checking the accuracy of his evaluations. This could be a problem if Barber misrepresented his findings in the research or if he left out key points in the argument about whether vampires exist. It is extremely difficult, sometimes impossible, to provide complete source information for research reviews. However, Barber might have strengthened his credibility by providing some references to allow you to do your own additional research on the topic or just to check his.

In addition, Barber himself is an expert on this subject. Woven into his research review, he gives his own expert opinion to prove his hypothesis that vampires do not exist. How do you know when his research review stops and his expert opinion starts? As previously discussed, experts can be incorrect. The way Barber has constructed his essay forces the reader to rely heavily on his methods of research and his own expert opinion. Questioning Barber on any of his points would force you to go out and do much of your own research on the topic to either prove Barber wrong or to ensure the reliability of his research.

But does Barber support his hypothesis? Absolutely! Ultimately, Barber has given you a point-by-point explanation, supported by scientific and psychological research, proving that eyewitness accounts of vampires can be explained by either natural, scientific, or psychological causes; thus, vampires, as the eyewitnesses saw them, do not exist. While you might have questions about how the evidence is handled or whether Barber's handling of it is thoroughly reliable, his piece is a successful example of how the evidence used needs to clearly support the hypothesis.

Step Four: Problems in Thinking About and Handling the Evidence

We have already discussed some of the difficulties both Mascetti and Barber encountered in handling the evidence in support of their hypotheses. Before you practice evaluating one of the selections in this book on your own, you should be aware that there are several specific problems that authors encounter when handling evidence, and these problems affect the strength of their arguments and the final reliability of their work. It is the responsibility of the author, and the reader as well, to be highly aware of these difficulties. Awareness of the particular challenges faced by both the reader and the author allows both individuals a greater chance of arriving at a more certain conclusion to their original question—in our case, whether vampires exist. We will look briefly at the types of problems with handling evidence.

Assumptions. Assumptions are statements accepted as true without proof. This problem is very dangerous because the chances of being incorrect are high. Regarding vampires, a writer might assume that vampires are a fiction and work only off of that assumption as opposed to solid research that proves they are not real. Assumptions lack evidence to prove their accuracy.

Either/or perspective. This line of thinking argues that something is either black or white. This perspective does not allow for shades of gray, compromise, or ambiguity. It is an extreme perspective with an all-or-nothing agenda that leaves no room for maybe, sometimes, or occasionally.

Absolutism. Absolutists have trouble seeing that there might be more than one way to look at the truth, that there are levels of complexity on certain issues that cannot be answered with a single *yes* or *no*. For example, an absolutist perspective on vampires might be that vampires absolutely do not exist in any way, shape, or form. This perspective would prevent the individual from seeing the alternative possibility that vampires could exist in different forms and to varying degrees.

Biased viewpoints. Simply put, to be biased is to be prejudiced toward a particular viewpoint. All people carry biases, some they are aware of and some they are not. In trying to develop a critical perspective, it is important to try to become aware of what your biases are. Also, you must consider the author's biases. Bias affects the way you process and perceive information and events. It often prevents you from seeing what is reasonable or truthful in evidence simply because you are biased against it. On the other hand, bias can prompt you to see truth in something that is incorrect or inaccurate simply because it agrees with your views. In addition, bias prevents authors from fully considering other viewpoints since they might feel that their view is the only correct one.

Judgments based on double standards. Sometimes people use one set of rules or criteria to judge something they agree with and a completely different set of rules to judge something they disagree with. This is called holding a double standard. If authors believe that vampires exist, they might hold evidence that argues for their existence to a different standard than evidence that proves they do not exist. Fairness and objectivity demand that both sides of the argument be given equal treatment and analysis. Holding double standards prevents this from happening.

Jumping to conclusions. Sometimes readers and authors make a conclusion or judgment on a topic without enough information or evidence to ensure that the conclusion is correct. Reading only one article that argues for the existence of vampires cannot provide enough evidence to conclude for certain that vampires exist. There are other perspectives, other evidence, and other ideas that should be evaluated before making up your mind.

Overgeneralizing. Sometimes people draw broad conclusions or make wide judgments with only a small amount of evidence. For example, you may have read in one essay that vampires live in coffins in the ground. From this, you conclude that this must be true of all vampires; however, it may not be. You cannot be certain of this because you have not done the research to find out whether this can be said of all vampires. Overgeneralizing limits the ability of the reader or author to see the entire picture presented by the evidence, thus making an accurate conclusion impossible.

Stereotyping. A stereotype is really a type of overgeneralization that is fixed in the mind of the person who holds it and is resistant to change. Stereotyping presents some of the same types of evidence-handling problems as overgeneralizing, but to a greater degree.

All of these challenges prohibit clear and critical thinking on a topic. They also prevent authors from thinking clearly about evidence and handling it appropriately in their writing. It is important to be aware that all people experience these barriers to critical thinking at various times, particularly when they have strong feelings about a topic. Overcoming these barriers will enable you to more clearly see all of the possible perspectives related to an issue and to handle the evidence you gather more objectively as you search for answers. As you evaluate the evidence presented by the authors in this book, pay attention to these challenges. Do you see any biased perspectives? Are authors considering possibilities or viewpoints other than their own? Are they basing their arguments on stereotypes or overgeneralizations? Have they jumped to any conclusions that are not supported by appropriate evidence? Also pay attention to these questions in relation to your own evaluation of what the writers are presenting to you. Are you drawing conclusions based on clear and objective evaluation of the evidence, or are you allowing yourself to fall victim to the problems described above?

Step Five: Forming a Conclusion About the Author's Hypothesis

We have examined the hypotheses of Mascetti and Barber, evaluated the evidence presented by them in support of their hypotheses, and looked at some of the problems the authors encounter in thinking and writing critically about whether vampires exist. It is time to form some conclusions about their hypotheses. Do they make sense? What do you think about the arguments presented by Mascetti and Barber? Who has a stronger case? What evidence have they presented that might help you to make up your mind about the existence of vampires? Is their evidence alone enough for you to make a decision? Or do you need additional information before coming to a conclusion? Are your judgments or conclusions free of biases and stereotypes that might prevent you from seeing their evidence clearly and making a solid judgment, even if that judgment is the opposite of what you have always believed about vampires?

Step Six: Practice What You Have Learned

Select one or more of the remaining ten articles from the book to evaluate on your own using the information in the steps outlined above. Since you are trying to determine whether vampires exist, you might consider selecting one piece from each side of the argument and evaluating them side by side. You can follow the format suggested below or make up one of your own. Just be sure to include all of the steps we learned above.

Name of article_____ Author_____

1. Examine the author's background and experience. What credentials does he or she hold that indicate that she or he has some expertise in the field of vampire studies? How might the author's experiences or expertise present problems in how the author perceives or handles evidence?

2. In one or two complete sentences, state the author's hypothesis in your own words. Be as specific as possible.

3a. In complete sentences, list the key points of evidence the author provides to support his or her hypothesis. You may want to create a numbered list since this will be easier to work with in the next step.

3b. Examine the evidence the author provides. For each key point of evidence you listed above, determine the type of evidence it is and evaluate whether it appears to be reliable and why. In general, do you believe the evidence provided by the author supports his or her hypothesis? Why?

4. Consider the challenges the author may be dealing with in handling and presenting the evidence. Does there appear to be any hasty conclusions, stereotypes, or overgeneralizations? How might the author be overly biased toward his or her perspective? Also, consider whether you are experiencing any of these challenges yourself in examining the author's work. What biases do you hold toward the author's perspective? Are you evaluating each side of the argument equally, or are you evaluating the side that you agree with differently than the opposing side? Examine and discuss the problems these challenges present to both the author's ability to convince you of his or her hypothesis and your ability to think critically about the issue.

5. Form a conclusion about the writer's hypothesis. How has the writer used evidence to adequately support his or her claim? How does the author's argument assist you in determining the truth about vampires? What conclusions can you reach based on the author's hypothesis and evidence? Do you feel your question can be fully answered based on your evaluation, or do you need to do more research? Explain.

Glossary

archetype: The original idea, image, or model after which other things are patterned; for example, the image of the vampire in the novel *Dracula* is an archetype for all other vampires.

contagion: A situation in which a disease is transmitted by contact with the infected body, air, or environment (i.e., contaminated river water); contagion occurs with transmission of such diseases as the plague, tuberculosis, or typhoid.

folklore: The traditional beliefs, practices, legends, and tales of a people that are passed from one generation to another through oral accounts.

forensic: Of or used in legal proceedings and public debate; often refers to medical or scientific evidence surrounding the processes of decomposition and crime-scene evidence.

group vampirism: A type of psychic vampirism that takes place among members of a group; this type of vampirism can be found within both informal and formal organizations.

host victim: The individual(s) chosen by the psychic vampire to provide the energy needed for the vampire to thrive; in contrast to blood donors, host victims are usually unaware that their energy is being used by the psychic vampire.

motif: A recurring theme found in a musical, literary, or artistic work; for example, the theme of loss and rebirth is a motif found in vampire fiction.

occultist: A person who studies the supernatural or believes in supernatural powers.

parasitic vampirism: An internal form of psychic vampirism in which the vampire turns against him or herself.

pathology: The scientific study of the nature of disease, also the ways in which a disease manifests itself within the body or the ways in which it functions.

pestilence: A fatal epidemic disease, especially referring to the bubonic plague.

photosensitive: Sensitive to light, especially sunlight.

porphyria: A metabolic blood disorder, usually hereditary, that may cause sensitivity to light, abdominal cramping, and the appearance of particular chemicals, called porphyrins, in the blood and urine that cause the urine to turn purple.

psychic vampirism: A form of vampirism that involves the draining of energy or life force from the host victim by the vampiric individual.

psychopathology: The study of the development or behavioral characteristics of a mental disorder.

vukodlak/volkodlak: A term for vampires used by the Slovenian people; it can also be used as a term for werewolves.

For Further Research

Nina Auerbach, *Our Vampires, Ourselves.* Chicago: University of Chicago Press, 1995.

Matthew Bunson, *The Vampire Encyclopedia.* New York: Gramercy Books, 1993.

Basil Copper, *The Vampire in Legend and Fact.* New York: Citadel/Carol, 1990.

Norine Dresser, *American Vampires: Fans, Victims, and Practitioners.* New York: W.W. Norton, 1989.

Alan Dundes, ed., *The Vampire: A Casebook.* Madison: University of Wisconsin Press, 1998.

Daniel Farson, *The Supernatural: Vampires, Zombies, and Monster Men.* London: Aldus Books, 1975.

Radu Florescu and Raymond T. McNally, *Dracula, Prince of Many Faces: His Life and Times.* Boston: Little, Brown, 1989.

Rosemary Ellen Guiley, *The Complete Vampire Companion.* New York: Macmillan, 1994.

Olga Hoyt, *Lust for Blood: The Consuming Story of Vampires.* Lanham, MD: Scarborough House, 1984.

Anthony Masters, *The Natural History of the Vampire.* London: Rupert Hart-Davis, 1972.

Raymond T. McNally, *A Clutch of Vampires.* New York: Bell, 1974.

Raymond T. McNally and Radu Florescu, *In Search of Dracula: The History of Dracula and Vampires.* New York: Houghton Mifflin, 1994.

J. Gordon Melton, *The Vampire Book: The Encyclopedia of the Undead.* Detroit: Visible Ink, 1994.

Gabriel Ronay, *The Truth About Dracula.* New York: Stein and Day, 1974.

Joe H. Slate, *Psychic Vampires: Protection from Energy Predators and Parasites.* St. Paul: Llewellyn, 2002.

Dudley Wright, *The Book of Vampires.* New York: Causeway Books, 1973.

Index